Eric Ambler was born into a family of entertainers and in his early years helped out as a puppeteer. However, he initially chose engineering as a full time career, although this quickly gave way to writing. In World War II he entered the army and looked likely to fight in the line, but was soon after commissioned and ended the war as assistant director of the army film unit and a Lieutenant-Colonel.

This experience translated into civilian life and Ambler had a very successful career as a screen writer, receiving an Academy Award for his work on *The Cruel Sea* by Nicolas Monsarrat in 1953. Many of his own works have been filmed, the most famous probably being *Light of Day*, filmed as *Topkapi* under which title it is now published.

He established a reputation as a thriller writer of extraordinary depth and originality and received many other accolades during his lifetime, including two *Edgar Awards* from *The Mystery Writers of America* (best novel for *Topkapi* and best biographical work for *Here Lies Eric Ambler),* and two *Gold Dagger Awards* from the *Crime Writer's Association (Passage of Arms* and *The Levanter).*

Often credited as being the inventor of the modern political thriller, *John Le Carre* once described Ambler as '*the source on which we all draw.*' A recurring theme in his works is the success of the well meaning yet somewhat bungling amateur who triumphs in the face of both adversity and hardened professionals.

Ambler wrote under his own name and also during the 1950's a series of novels as *Eliot Reed*, with *Charles Rhodda.* These are now published under the '*Ambler*' umbrella.

Works of **ERIC AMBLER** published by
HOUSE OF STRATUS

DOCTOR FRIGO
JUDGMENT ON DELTCHEV
THE LEVANTER
THE SCHIRMER INHERITANCE
THE SIEGE OF THE VILLA LIPP   (Also as 'Send No More Roses')
TOPKAPI   (Also as 'The Light Of Day')

Originally as Eliot Reed with Charles Rhodda:
CHARTER TO DANGER
THE MARAS AFFAIR
PASSPORT TO PANIC
TENDER TO DANGER   (Also as 'Tender To Moonlight')
SKYTIP

Autobiography:
HERE LIES ERIC AMBLER

Charter to Danger

eric *Ambler*

(Writing as Eliot Reed with Charles Rhodda)

HOUSE OF
STRATUS

This edition published in 2009 by House of Stratus, an imprint of Stratus Books Ltd., 21 Beeching Park, Kelly Bray, Cornwall, PL17 8QS, UK.

www.houseofstratus.com

Typeset, printed and bound by House of Stratus.

A catalogue record for this book is available from the British Library and the Library of Congress.

ISBN 0-7551-2380-8
EAN 978-0-7551-2380-3

Chapter 1

The card bore the name of F. Caton Margolies. It was beautifully printed and came from a handsome leather wallet with platinum adornments. Well, conceivably platinum.

Ross Barnes raised his eyes from the thin glinting metalwork to meet the attending, incurious gaze of Mr. Margolies. The hands that held the wallet had long slender fingers, flexible, smooth as if they had been sandpapered. You might imagine those fingers drifting idly over the keyboard of a piano or closing the stops of a flageolet. Nothing more arduous.

"Would it be inconvenient if I suggested an immediate inspection of the craft?"

The tone, like the words, carried a suggestion of innate courtesy. Or of a tradition of good manners. Beacon Hill? Certainly Boston; and certainly most genteel.

Ross Barnes was used to an easier, more idiomatic American; but his experience had been limited to the rough and tumble of bridge-heads on forlorn beaches or the hasty hospitality of wardrooms under conditions of active service. He had liked those Americans; had got on well with them. Not that he wasn't getting on well enough with Mr. Margolies. It was merely that he found so much gentility a shade oppressive. It may have been because of this that there was a grudging note in his reply.

"She's not what I'd call shipshape, but you can look her over if you like."

Mr. Margolies smiled. "I might remark that I am empowered by my principal to conclude arrangements, if, in my judgment, everything is satisfactory."

It was a nice smile. It gave a touch of warmth to a frank, pleasant face. Only in the grey-green eyes was there a last reserve. Possibly Mr. Margolies could not descend entirely from the rarefied atmosphere in which he moved. To be private secretary to Croesus was to walk with Croesus and see the world from a somewhat elevated point of view.

Ross Barnes said: "Well, let's get on with it, shall we?"

He picked his way through the marine litter of the repair yards and so round the head of the slip where a couple of hands were working on a twenty-foot yacht. Margolies followed him to the small pier where a long, compact little vessel lay, her new paint-work gleaming in the mild sunlight of the morning.

"You will readily appreciate that I would scarcely have come to Portsmouth if a final decision was not within my scope," Margolies remarked, stepping gingerly. "Mr. Flavius found the specifications quite satisfactory."

"Is Mr. Flavius still in London?"

Margolies deprecated with a gesture a question, so crudely direct. "Mr. Flavius," he said, "is at the moment travelling incognito. He will remain incognito until his arrival in Cannes next month. Incidentally, if I should decide in favour of your craft, the arrangement is to be regarded as a top secret."

"Why?" Ross Barnes halted to look at his visitor.

Mr. Margolies condescended to explain. "For his personal comfort Mr. Flavius wishes to avoid publicity. It is only when he comes to Europe that he can enjoy the privacy that is the daily privilege of the common man."

"I see. I thought it might have something to do with this merger business. I was reading in one of the papers . . . ."

"Mr. Barnes! Please!" The reproof was marked by a rather anxious frown, and the subject was changed with haste. "I understand you will yourself take charge of your vessel?"

"That's the idea." Ross Barnes shrugged. "I'm making it my job, my business."

"You were, I believe, an officer in the British Navy?"

"Lieutenant. Royal Navy."

"Of course, I beg your pardon." Mr. Margolies was distressed by the hint that he had committed a solecism. "Possibly," he went on, gesturing towards the newly painted craft, "you served in this sort of thing?"

"Not quite. I was in destroyers."

"Ah, destroyers! What was this originally, an M.T.B.?"

"No. H.D.M.L. Motor launch for harbour defence. The torpedo boat job was quite a bit larger."

"Forgive me. I am not too familiar with this type of craft. I spent the war years mainly on the other side, and in a coastguard cutter."

The long pale fingers of Mr. Margolies moved as if they were stopping the frets of a - well, of a coastguard cutter. Ross Barnes made no comment. He merely took a quick glance at Mr. Margolies. Strange things happened in a war.

But these were the humdrum days of peace and a man had to make a living.

"Mind the paint on the superstructure," Ross said.

Margolies stepped from the pier to the spotless deck and went forward carefully. He was interested. He asked questions. He inspected everything; the miniature bridge, the cubby-hole chart-house, the relatively spacious saloon, the sleeping-cabins, the bathrooms, the galley, the fuel tanks, the Diesels.

"Gardners!" he remarked, astonishingly, as if he had come across old friends. "Are they in good shape?"

"On the top line," Barnes answered. "They've been thoroughly overhauled."

Margolies lingered, stroking metal parts caressingly with his musician's fingers.

"They are nice," he said. "Everything is nice. I congratulate you on an excellent conversion."

"Then you think she will do?"

"Nothing could be better for the job." Mr. Margolies wrenched his eyes from the engines and cast an appraising glance over other details.

"How many guests will Mr. Flavius be having?"

"That is not yet determined, but you have no need to be anxious, Mr. Barnes. The accommodation is ample for all requirements. And I may say that Mr. Flavius does not wish for a larger or more elaborate craft. He always avoids ostentation. How soon will you be ready to sail?"

"Within a few days."

"Will it be possible for you to arrive in Cannes on the fifteenth of next month?"

"That's more time than I need."

Mr. Margolies smiled. "I am not now thinking of your time, Mr. Barnes. We require you to be in Cannes on the fifteenth and not a day earlier. How you contrive it, is your business. We accept the terms you mentioned in your letter to the agent. We will compensate you if you think our date means a loss of time to you."

Barnes shook his head. "The fifteenth suits me. I'll take her down to the Mediterranean by easy stages. I want to settle her down. Get everything trim."

Mr. Margolies nodded approvingly. "What crew will you carry?" he asked.

"I'll manage with an engineer and a boy till I get to Cannes."

"Good. You may leave the rest to me. Mr. Flavius will have some of his personal staff to take care of him. If I should have any instructions for you, I shall address them in care of the American Express at Marseilles. On the other hand, you must inform me at once should you meet with any accident or delaying mishap. During the period of our incognito I shall be known as Benjamin Field. The Cannes post office will take care of any mail in that name. Is there anything else?"

"I don't know." Ross hesitated. One felt a little diffident about mentioning small change when dealing with Vincent J. Flavius or his representative. "I've certain bills to clear before I sail. The business details . . ."

Mr. Margolies jumped at the cue. "The business details will be settled immediately. You understand, of course, we might have secured a yacht that was already on the spot? We have, in fact, been looking out for one, but Mr. Flavius was attracted by your advertisement, especially as you undertook to make your craft available at a French Riviera port."

Was this the preliminary to a haggling bout?

Ross, meeting the grey-green gaze, answered a little sharply. "Naturally the voyage to Cannes is my responsibility. I don't expect you to hire me from here. My aim is to get established on the Riviera. The agent should have made that quite clear."

"So long as it is quite clear between us." Mr. Margolies smiled reassuringly. "The chance that brought your advertisement before us was probably a most happy one. I'll have your agent make out the charter party at once, and a deposit will be handed over to you on signature. Will that be satisfactory?"

"Entirely."

"The full amount to be paid in sterling?"

"Half would be better. You could arrange for the rest in francs. I'll need currency for re-fuelling on the canals. There'll be river pilotage, too."

"You mean you're planning to make the trip by the canals and down the Rhône?" Arched brows pointed the question.

"Yes."

"No, Mr. Barnes. Decidedly no." The tone now was harshly emphatic. "We would much prefer you to make the passage by sea."

Ross was disconcerted. "I don't know that I can face the additional expense. The fuel consumption would be quite an item. And there would be currency difficulties."

Mr. Margolies hesitated. There was, perhaps, some small question of decency in spending another man's money but in a fraction of time his brow cleared.

"Let us help you, Mr. Barnes. Your craft is so admirably suitable, I am not disposed to be put off by a little extra expense."

"I might advertise for a passenger or two."

"No." Mr. Margolies was emphatic again. "We want no complications. When will you be ready to sail?"

"Next week."

"Then we'll charter you from next week. You will accept a nominal sum for the voyage to the Mediterranean, since we will not be using you until you reach Cannes. We will undertake to arrange and pay for bunkering facilities at, say, Lisbon, Gibraltar, Barcelona. And Marseilles. That will leave you to take care of things as far as Brest. I'll go into the monetary considerations with your agent and make sure that you are not out of pocket. Definitely."

"But surely the bunkering will mean a lot of trouble for you?"

"None at all, Mr. Barnes. For your part, you'll be able to manage with your engineer and your boy on coasting runs. You'll still have plenty of time. You would not save so much on the inland course because you would have to bring up at night."

"I've allowed for all that."

"No doubt. But Mr. Flavius would not like it if you went through the canals. There is so much traffic. And a craft like yours would be conspicuous. Yes, conspicuous." Mr. Margolies brought the tips of his slender fingers together in a prayerful gesture. "You will take the sea route, please. Otherwise it might get out that you were under charter to Mr. Flavius. No, no, no. He wouldn't like that at all, Mr. Barnes."

Mr. Barnes shrugged. Mr. Flavius was possibly a little over-sensitive, but this was no time to quibble. Mr. Margolies was offering gingerbread and there was quite a lot of gilt on it; more than one could reasonably have expected.

Ross relaxed, grinning amiably. He wondered if he should suggest a drink at the local across from the yard, just to clinch the deal, but before he could express the thought Mr. Margolies killed it.

"You will forgive me if I seem a little abrupt," that gentleman murmured. "I am in a hurry to get back to London. Officially, I leave by air for the Continent to join Mr. Flavius to-night. Actually, I shall remain to settle the charter party, but I shall be at a different hotel."

"Incognito?"

"Precisely."

They were on the pier again, walking towards the gates of Judson's yard. Mr. Margolies turned and glanced at the gleaming white craft as though he had forgotten something.

"By the way," he said, "I don't notice any name. What are you going to call her?"

"*Roselle.*"

"How very nice! After your wife, perhaps?"

"I'm not married," said Ross shortly.

"Ah, then, your fiancée perhaps ? I seem to detect a matter of sentiment. Don't tell me I'm wrong?"

"Not entirely." Ross Barnes halted at the exit to the roadway. "The name runs in the family. My father used to win races with a dinghy called *Roselle.*"

"So we progress!" Mr. Margolies laughed pleasantly and held out his hand. "I shall watch for *Roselle* on the fifteenth of next month. Bon voyage, Mr. Barnes. *Bon voyage.*"

Chapter 2

Afterwards, when he looked back on it, it all seemed slick and beautifully contrived. Mr. Margolies had angled shrewdly for the information he needed to satisfy himself of the dependability of Ross Barnes. The little vessel was speedy, she had reliable engines and big fuel tanks. The owner – who was also her skipper – was a free agent. Undoubtedly *Roselle* would arrive on the due date.

But Ross Barnes had no feeling that Mr. Margolies had been more than normally calculating – normally, that is, for a representative of the legendary Mr. Flavius. Certainly he had found nothing in the interview to cause him any anxiety. For an hour or so after the departure of the visitor, in fact, Ross was quite busy being pleased with himself. Luck was with him. His first advertisement in *The Times* had brought him a client. And what a client! One of the wealthiest of all the international tycoons, the fabulous Flavius himself. And one charter might lead to others. It was well known that Mr. Flavius visited the French Riviera every year, and Mr. Flavius had never bothered about owning yachts. He preferred oil wells and steel mills and chemical plants. So it was not inconceivable that Ross would get the job of carrying him round the Mediterranean whenever he had the taste for a cruise.

Meanwhile there was that change in the sailing plan, but it was of no particular moment. Elation prevailed.

"Juddy," Ross addressed the head of the yard; "you may put that extra gear in the chain locker. I can afford it now. Have Bert give her the final lick as soon as she'll take it. We'll be sailing next week. I'll let you have another cheque when I've overhauled the account."

"We'll be sailing next week." He repeated the information to Eleanor, his sister, and to Tom Peters, Eleanor's husband, when he returned to London in the evening.

"You'll have to make up your mind about young Ralph," he warned Eleanor. "If he's not to come with us, I'll have to find another boy at once. There'll be lots to do before we sail."

From the day the ex-harbour defence craft became the property of Ross Barnes, young Ralph Peters had constantly dreamed of making a trip in her, and now the opportunity was here. He had finished school. He had nothing particular to do until he was called up for service in a month or two, and surely there could be no brighter a preliminary than a voyage with an uncle who had always been the exemplar of the ideal life, the very model of the modern naval officer, the handsome, dashing lieutenant whose exploits had brought him resounding fame - in the family circle.

Ross might have resisted the more glowing epithets, but Ross, in the view of the youth, was essentially a modest man.

It had always been difficult to draw from him the details of a career that had ranged from the frozen Baltic to the sunny strand of Anzio, but the details that Ralph had gleaned he treasured and enlarged. At eighteen years, hero-worship had passed its peak. Now the remote idol had become a warm and amiable person whose human qualities had suffered nothing in their maturing. He was still the model, trim and athletic in figure, neat in dress, with frankness in his lean, well-formed face, stubbornness in the cut of his jaw, firmness without hardness in the line of his mouth, decision in his brow, and humour and understanding in his fine grey eyes.

Ralph wondered why such an uncle could ever have brought himself to relinquish a career that might have offered an apotheosis in much gold braid. Ross could have told him, but largely, perhaps, it was a matter of temperament. Ross had not pursued his opportunities for advancement. He had wanted to be out on his own, independent. He had nothing to say against the Navy. He favoured it whole-heartedly as the immediate destination, if not the destiny, of his nephew. There was no better training for a young man of Ralph's inclinations, and the voyage of *Roselle* would afford an easy induction to the sea.

He made the latter belief clear when Eleanor, pained by the thought of the imminent parting, began to demur in a mother's way.

Ralph, with his bag secretly packed, listened in agony. Women!

"I don't know that I like it," Eleanor said. "He'll be going away from us for a long time so very soon. Surely he'll have enough of the sea in the Navy? And this craft of yours is so small, Ross, for such a voyage. Just a cockleshell. I'll be afraid for him all the time."

"Nonsense!" Tom Peters answered her. "Anybody would think Ross didn't know how to handle his job. What harm could come to the boy in such safe hands?"

Eleanor became absurd. "He's never been from home before. He needs so much looking after."

"I suppose you're planning to go along with him when he joins the Navy?"

"Don't be ridiculous, Tom!" Eleanor tried a line of retreat. "This is a different thing altogether. Ross is staying on the Riviera. Who's going to bring Ralph home?"

"Good heavens!" Her husband threw up his hands. "A big hobbledehoy of eighteen! He can get on a train, can't he?"

"But a French train! You don't know what will happen to him!"

Ross intervened. "You'll not have to worry, Eleanor. I'll put him on a plane at Nice and you can meet him at London Airport. He's set on coming with me, and it will really do him the world of good."

"Of course it will." Tom Peters was emphatic. "He'll be able to brush up his French, too."

"You're sure there's no danger?" Eleanor appealed to her brother.

"Not the slightest." Ross laughed. "My *Roselle* is as seaworthy as the *Queen Mary*. And we'll be keeping one foot on shore all the way. You let him come, Eleanor. He'll be safe, I promise you."

"All right."

Eleanor was still doubtful, but she had yielded and would not go back on her word.

Ross got on a bus and went to clinch matters with the other

member of his crew.

Tiny Kane had no one to consult. He was alone in the world, and that, perhaps, was why he just puttered round as a garage mechanic. The Navy had given him an overdose of the sea, but now he was fed up with tending to the needs of ailing cars and the land in turn had lost its attraction for him.

"When you go back, I go back with you," he had told Ross. "But no more of that blasted Navy. You can tell their lordships what they can do with it."

Ross had been inclined to defend the Admiralty. "Their lordships sold me a very nice craft."

"You let me know when you've had it fumigated."

Tiny Kane was fond of Ross Barnes. He was also fond of Diesel engines - so fond that they sometimes seemed to be the sum of his emotional life. He was a big man, as the name conferred on him by the Home Fleet might indicate. He was a very big man for a small engine-room, but Ross had been determined from the first to fit him in. Ross had been keeping a sometimes critical eye on him in port and he knew that Tiny Kane needed *Roselle*. That *Roselle* needed Tiny was a secondary matter. The big man had watched the conversion with increasing interest. He had gone down to Portsmouth on his days off and worked on the engines. Now he was eager for the day of departure, though he showed no great eagerness when Ross came to him with a definite proposal.

"The fumigation has been completed," Ross reported. "We go aboard on Monday."

"I'd better bring some D.D.T. along, anyway."

"What about your job?"

"I don't have to give notice. I can leave on Saturday. What's the plan?"

Ross told him. "We'll go to Brest by easy stages. Give you a chance to get used to the engines," he added. "Then we'll take the Bay on a straight course for Corunna. After that, we coast. Should be a fairly comfortable trip."

"Who is this Flavius chap?" Mr. Kane, who believed that man was born to sorrow, distrusted comfort. "How do you know he's genuine?"

"Vincent J. Flavius? I thought everybody knew about him."

"I don't," said Mr. Kane austerely. "Sounds like one of Nero's pals to me."

"Flavius is a simplification of a foreign name. I believe his family came from somewhere in the Balkans originally. Now, he's one of the richest bankers in the world. He's got millions."

"Yes, and how did he make them?"

Ross laughed. "Don't worry, Tiny," he said. "We'll have money in the kitty before we sail."

"Sucker money," Mr. Kane lamented. "A bit of the old come-on stuff while they're looking over your shirt." He rubbed fingers and thumb together as if he were testing a fabric. "Bankers! I wouldn't trust one farther than I could throw a depth charge. What a racket!"

"Where do you keep your money? Under the mattress?"

"You can laugh. You're too honest, Mr. Barnes. You'd trust anybody. But don't tell me later on that I didn't warn you."

Ross laughed again. And next day, when he thought of Tiny Kane, he was still amused, though he had to agree that there were certain aspects of the deal with Mr. Margolies that might be questioned by a very suspicious mind.

Certainly no doubts could be entertained about the agent. The reputation of K. Denishall Jackson was irreproachable. Mr. Margolies might be a little mysterious and Mr. Flavius a shade eccentric, but there was nothing to worry about in that. People who could afford to charter yachts were entitled to eccentricities. All the same, a word with Mr. Jackson himself could do no harm, and, early in the afternoon, Ross decided to call and have that word.

"I never heard of a Mr. Margolies," Mr. Jackson asserted.

Ross sat bolt upright.

"But you sent him to see my craft!"

"You have the wrong name, Mr. Barnes. The gentleman we sent to you was a Mr. Field - Benjamin Field."

Of course! The pseudonym! Mr. Margolies had disclosed himself to no one but the owner.

The agent had little information about Mr. Field, but that little was good. A man of character and decision, undoubtedly. He had been most favourably impressed by *Roselle* and was anxious to secure her. "We have now been furnished with a most adequate bank reference," Mr. Jackson added. "It seems that Mr. Field is not very well known socially in this country, but he has submitted American and French introductions. If you wish me to make further inquiries, I will do so. However, as our payment is assured, I don't think there is anything to worry about. The bank reference is most adequate."

Observing that his client seemed satisfied, Mr. Jackson turned to other matters. "I understand that you are to be in control of your ship, so the contract will not be by demise. I take it you are aware of the distinction between the terms 'by demise' and 'not by demise.' In this case you will be undertaking all the liabilities and duties of owner."

"I prefer it that way. It's my plan to run my own ship."

"Now that you are here, perhaps we could go into the details. Mr. Field is in great haste to conclude the formalities, so it may facilitate matters if I know your mind."

They went into the details. Since Mr. Margolies had kept the veil drawn, Ross was careful not to mention the name of Mr. Flavius, but in the evening he called on a Fleet Street friend, and asked a few questions. He had been a little disturbed by Mr. Field's deception of the chartering agent, and he felt that he must have more information.

It was true, he learned, that Vincent J. Flavius had been in London quite recently. Rumours of a big business deal had been persistent, but nothing authentic had leaked out. A curious fellow, Mr. Flavius. Quite a pleasant old boy, if you could get to him, but he hated publicity and shunned newspaper men. Perhaps it was just that he liked to be left alone. Anyway, it was a trick of his to travel under assumed names, though such a celebrity could not hope to hide his movements for long. Just now he was on an annual pilgrimage that usually wound up in the South of France and no doubt he would soon be heard of on the Riviera, where he had many friends.

It was all quite reassuring.

"Why are you so interested?" the journalist asked.

"Just thinking of business prospects," Ross answered.

"Then you can strike Flavius off the list. Nothing will ever get him on the sea. He hates it. He always travels by air."

"Well, you never know. He might like a trip round the Lérins on a calm day."

"Not if all they say about him is true."

Ross shrugged. He was not going to be disturbed by the sayings of the unnamed They. Myths could so easily be built up on a casual word or two. The trails of the mighty were cluttered with them.

"By the way," Ross said. "Do you happen to know the name of his secretary?"

"Which secretary? He has so many. There's a sort of personal aide who trots round with him and keeps everybody at a distance. Does it in a very agreeable way, too. Smart as a whip. Used to be a newspaper man."

"Do you know his name?"

"Yes. Margolies. Caton Margolies."

So that, too, was all right.

Ross Barnes shook off his last unreasonable doubt and went home to sleep soundly.

Next day the charter party was signed.

"Mr. Field regrets that he had no time to see you again," Denishall Jackson explained. "He looks forward to your arrival at Cannes. Everything is in order except for your signature. On each copy, please. Thank you. Here is our cheque for the sterling amount you stipulated. According to your agreement with Mr. Field, the balance will be conveyed to you in francs through Lloyds Bank in Cannes. We. of course, can accept no direct responsibility for that. However, our commission on the full amount involved has been covered. So, Mr. Barnes, there is nothing left for me but to wish you a happy voyage. Unless you will permit me to express the hope that we may be of service to you in the future. We shall be very happy to keep *Roselle* on our list of craft available in the Medit . . ."

He broke off suddenly, snapped his fingers and began feverishly to paw over the litter of files, blue prints and correspondence on his desk.

He uttered an exclamation of satisfaction as he came up with a long manilla envelope. "Yes, here we are! I had almost forgotten. Here are notes of instruction to the different firms who will see to your bunkering requirements. Corunna, Lisbon, Gibraltar, Barcelona, Marseilles. Mr. Field seems to be an excellent organiser. Leaves nothing to chance, does he? Quite a nice little charter, eh, Mr. Barnes? Quite nice."

Mr. Barnes recalled the different inflection Mr. Margolies had given to the adjective. Nice? Well, the contract was in his pocket and the money would be in the bank before three o'clock. And from now on, the good ship *Roselle* was bound, though not by demise, to fulfil the lawful orders of Mr. Field, unless prevented by Act of God, the Queen's Enemies, fire, and all and every other dangers and accidents of the seas, rivers, and navigation of whatever nature and kind soever.

Yes. On the whole, "nice" was probably the word.

Chapter 3

The voyage to the Mediterranean began auspiciously.

During *Roselle's* trials, Ross had had little opportunity of discovering how she handled in bad weather, but by the time they dropped anchor at Le Havre, their first port of call, he knew that she was everything he had hoped. Her engines had earned the unqualified, though grudging, approval of Tiny Kane. The French customs official who gave them clearance had flattering things to say of her internal appointments. By the time they reached Brest, even young Ralph Peters, who, during the first few days, had had some difficulty in acquiring his sea-legs, had succumbed to *Roselle's* sturdy charms. If, thereafter, he had a regret about this new life, it was only that he could not be on the bridge and in the engine-room at the same time.

Ross was very fond of his nephew and kept a careful eye on him. He had had some doubts, at first, about Kane's attitude. The engineer had grumbled a bit about taking a raw boy along, and prophesied disasters which stopped just short of Ralph's being swallowed by a whale. Certain it was that Biscay would raise a wave to wash him overboard; but before they came to the passage of that disreputable sea, Kane had evolved a heavily paternal attitude towards the youngster and spent all his spare time in making a sailor of him.

Ralph was a quick and attentive pupil, whether the lessons took him among the pots and pans of the cramped galley or the maps and tables of the little chart-house, where Ross had to correct or modify some of Mr. Kane's wilder navigational theories. But in galley or engine-room Kane was in undisputed authority. He could make a sea-pie with the best of them, and a Diesel under his caresses would sit up and purr.

Kane was an exact, even pedantic instructor, though his way of doing things was often exclusively his own. In laundry work, for instance. When you were required to hang out a shirt on the line rigged for drying, you had to observe a precise and particular method. You pegged it by the shoulders, turned each sleeve twice round the line, and then pegged the cuffs.

The effect, when the article became inflated by the wind, appealed to Ralph's sense of humour. He became convulsed. Ross was called to inspect the comic spectacle.

"Tiny says it's the way they hang out shirts in the Navy. Is that true?" Ralph demanded.

"No one ever hung out a shirt that way except Tiny himself," Ross told him. "And he never did it before to-day. He's pulling your leg, Ralph."

"I'm not," Kane protested solemnly. "Once when we were in Aden, I had a shirt blown clean away, and an Arab showed me the knack of it. The Arabs always twist the sleeves round the line when they hang up those nightshirt things they wear. Later on, there were so many shirts lost, the Admiralty took it up. You'll find it in Orders."

"Under 'Arab's nightshirt,' no doubt?"

Kane shrugged in pretended indignation. Ralph was doubled up. Ross retired, grinning.

"Ralph is having a wonderful time," he wrote to Eleanor from Brest. "And just as I told you, the trip is doing him the world of good. We have had sun all the way, and he is already so tanned, you wouldn't know him. Lest you still have qualms about these wicked foreign ports, I can assure you that he is well protected. Every time he goes ashore, Tiny goes with him as bodyguard and will not let him out of sight, so you see, my dear . . ."

Knowing how reluctant she had been to let Ralph go, Ross was at pains to show her that she had acted wisely in consenting. He had been a little worried about her, and he hastened to mail the letter, as if the act could finally relieve her anxiety.

And now they had come to the end of their leisurely days. They were off early in the morning and committed to Biscay.

Kane recanted his direful prophecies. "Perhaps it won't be so bad," he said. And it wasn't. There was a swell and that was all. *Roselle* took it in her stride and reached her first Spanish port a day ahead of plan.

After that they sailed by the calendar, coasting by long stages down to Gibraltar and up the Mediterranean to reach Marseilles with one day to spare. Nothing had marred their easy progress. The prearranged fuelling facilities had worked beautifully. Mr. Margolies had neglected nothing.

Now, at Marseilles, Ross found a letter of welcome waiting for him at the American Express office. Mr. Margolies had to say that the arrangements were to be altered slightly. The *Roselle* was required to arrive at Cannes on the sixteenth, not the fifteenth, and she was to be brought into the port between five and six in the evening.

It seemed that incognito, secrecy, concealment, whatever was the appropriate term, was more important than ever. A business deal involving vast sums was about to be concluded, and it might be necessary to use *Roselle* as a meeting-place. Every move was being watched by opposing interests, as fortunes might be won or lost by informed anticipation. Unfortunately it was being rumoured that "a certain party" had chartered a yacht, so it was more than ever important that no suspicion should attach to *Roselle*.

Mr. Barnes was to wait on board until eight o'clock in the evening. If no message reached him by that time, he was to go to the *Café des Lauriers* in the Suquet, order a drink or something to eat, and there Mr. Margolies would join him and transmit to him an amended plan.

In conclusion, Mr. Margolies wished to impress on Mr. Barnes that he must keep the fuel tanks full, as it might be necessary to sail at a moment's notice to pick up a guest at a distant point. If Mr. Margolies suggested that this point might be Rapallo, Mr. Barnes should take it as purely hypothetical, because the last detail would not be known till the eleventh hour.

Mr. Barnes frowned. It was all rather childish. The letter was typewritten on a plain quarto sheet. There was no address on it and it was signed Benj. Field. The envelope bore the imprint of the *Hotel Edouard Lanneau*, Nice, but that, of course, did not mean a thing. Unless it meant that "a certain party" was moving about a bit.

The Mediterranean was really blue that morning. Ross cancelled the frown with a laugh. Perhaps these strange manoeuvres were necessary in the game of high finance. In any case, there was no point in taking them seriously. Mr. Flavius had engaged to pay liberally for his charter, so he was entitled to cut a few capers. Ross rather looked forward to meeting the old boy.

Pushing the letter and torn envelope into a pocket of his jacket, he walked out into the sun and made his way back towards the yacht basin. On the way he bought newspapers, and later, in one of them, he saw a few lines recording that a visitor to Nice had been identified as M. Vincent Flavius. It was understood that Mr. Flavius was staying at the *Hotel Edouard Lanneau,* but would go on to Cannes in a few days.

So that checked up. Still, there was a leakage somewhere. Wall Street was probably in a state of consternation. Mr. Margolies would be most displeased.

Chapter 4

Cannes. The sun was down behind the Estérel and the line of that sea-seeking range was drawn hard against the last light in the west.

It was very nice, as Mr. Margolies might have remarked had he been there. Everything timed to the minute; formalities taken care of, oil in the tanks, moorings secure, and the crew ready to cast off at the drop of a flag.

Ross, having stepped ashore, looked back at his small ship with pride. She was in elegant company. The *Albert-Édouard* Jetty was a millionaires' row of gleaming pleasure craft, crowded together beam to beam, most of them imposingly be-funnelled, with here and there a ketch or a cutter, and, at the seaward end, a tall-masted auxiliary schooner with a sleek dark hull.

Some of them were habituées. Some of them Ross knew, for he had spent a season here as the hired skipper of a typical specimen, an experience that had turned his thoughts to ownership. She was there, his old charge, along the line towards the Croisette, She had the stamp of luxury on every ring-bolt, but she had never given him the satisfaction that he had from his new love.

Roselle was his own creation, and he felt that he had good reason to be proud of her. Certainly she could take her place in the company. She was spotless, scrubbed and polished till you could eat off any part of her, and she was fit for any Flavius, however fabulous.

Ross walked along the jetty. There must be people here he knew, but he saw no one he recognised. No one stirred on the pleasure-craft. The whole row seemed dead and abandoned and strollers on the jetty were few. Mr. Margolies was not in sight, and no messenger came. Ross returned to *Roselle.*

Ralph was giving a last wipe to the paintwork of the davits on the port side. When he had finished he stepped round the stern of the dinghy and gazed across the harbour at the old town.

There had been no end of wonder for the boy in all the ports they had touched at. There was no end now. His eyes reached to the snow-tipped wall of the mountains beyond Grasse, then came back to the dusky hills round the port.

"I'd like to be staying on," he told Ross. "It has been such a wonderful voyage."

"There'll be a bit more of it for you when we get our orders. We may even be off again to-night. Too bad, isn't it?"

Ross grinned. He felt happy. A stage was completed and he could relax until the orders arrived.

The flush of the afterglow was almost gone and the peaks of the Estérel would soon be lost in the night. Lights spangled the shore line, shining through the trees of the Allées.

Ross looked at his watch, then re-read the letter he had picked up in Marseilles.

Eight o'clock. The *Café des Lauriers* in the Suquet.

It still wanted some minutes to seven.

He knew the café in the Suquet. It was not the sort of place to gain laurels from guidebook editors, but he had used it sometimes when francs had been short. He wondered why on earth the elegant Mr. Margolies had selected such a joint.

The appeal, no doubt, was to the conspirator. The appropriate dress, possibly, was a cloak. Daggers would be worn.

Ralph said: "What are you laughing at?"

"Just a thought."

Ross went to his cabin to get some money from a tin box under his bunk.

He waited, but still there was no word from Margolies.

When it was time, he stepped to the galley where Tiny was cooking supper. "I'll have to keep that date ashore," he announced. "Wait here till I get back. Then you and Ralph will be able to take a look at the town, I hope."

"Aye, aye, sir." Tiny was very pleased with himself or his cooking. "What about your meal?"

"I'll get something."

At the end of the jetty Ross halted. Quite a few people were moving between the Allées and the entrance to the old Casino, and some were heading towards the jetty. Margolies might, of course, be late. Better give him a minute or two.

The pause was stretched to five minutes, but no one resembling Mr. Margolies appeared among the promenaders. The only figure that seemed at all familiar was a man in a knot of loungers at the corner of the Casino. The seaman's *maillot*, the loose jacket, the peaked white cap crushed carelessly down on an over-large head recalled a Russian named Varenine who had settled in Cannes, but when Ross took a step nearer, he saw that it was not Max Varenine. The man stared at him for a moment, then turned to talk to a companion, a stoop-shouldered young fellow who held his head forward as if there were something wrong with his neck.

Ross walked on. He was crossing the Allées towards the Rue Félix Faure when he felt vaguely uneasy.

It might be the anxiety of a stranger in a strange land, yet he was no stranger here. He knew every plane tree of the Allées and every twist and turn he must take to the little café, where he would find old Berthe at the cash-desk and surely some acquaintance from the Quai St. Pierre among the customers. Cannes did not change so much in a couple of years.

He half turned to glance over his shoulder. From the *Hotel de Ville* he glanced back again. Almost as if he had a notion that he was being followed.

Preposterous, of course. He was imagining things. Prompted by his employer, Margolies might go to ridiculous lengths to preserve an incognito, but there had to be a limit to eccentricity. The idea that Margolies could have been watching for him and was now following him was quite beyond reason.

Ross went on and found the narrow, climbing street that led to his objective. He saw the dull orange glow of the windows, and, in the light of a bracket lamp fixed to the building opposite, he could read the sign-board. He looked for the foliage of an oleander that reached out over a tall wall within the range of the street-lamp. It was there. He told himself that nothing had changed. But he was wrong.

The *Café des Lauriers* was different. It had always been a dingy place; now it was dirty. It looked as if it had been badly treated and was sulkily resigned to a dismal end. Berthe was gone from the cash-desk. A ponderous, black-bearded fellow in shirt-sleeves stood at the little bar just inside the doorway. A new proprietor? He had an unhappy scowl on his face, and the arrival of a customer did not remove it.

He said, "Monsieur?" in an aggressive sort of way.

The unexpected changes had disconcerted Ross. He looked down the long dull room at the little tables, the battered cane chairs. The furnishings were familiar but the stage of dilapidation they had now reached was almost final. Two tables were occupied by tough lads who argued loudly across the floor. About food or a woman, or both.

Ross nodded to the bearded man and sat down at one of the cleaner tables.

A girl came from the kitchen with immense unconcern. Ross ordered coffee and a *fine*. He was hungry, but that could wait.

The coffee arrived promptly.

"Where is Berthe?" he asked the girl.

A shrug. "She has gone. You knew her?"

"I knew her. Does Max Varenine still come here?"

She was puzzled by the name.

"Russian Max," Ross prompted.

Blackbeard, leaning forward across his zinc bar, intervened.

"We are not communists here."

Ross, remembering the virulent whiteness of Max, grinned. "I congratulate you."

The street door swung open and a new customer paused at the zinc. Expecting Margolies, Ross looked round quickly, and was startled to recognise the newcomer as one of the men he had seen by the old

Casino, the stoop-shouldered one with the wry neck. The man called for a drink, then looked down the room as if seeking someone. His glance took in Ross and passed on. He was a handsome young fellow but rather frail and with a suggestion of effeminacy. There was something peculiar about his eyes as well as his neck. They were large and lustrous, but set deeply in dark-ringed sockets. He drank down his wine, pushed his glass across the zinc, and crossed to the telephone opposite the bar.

Ross stared. He had seen the man at the end of the jetty and now he was seeing him again at the telephone in the *Café des Lauriers*. A coincidence? Merely a coincidence? Or was the call being made to inform Margolies that the owner of *Roselle* had come ashore?

There was no box round the telephone. Ross listened intently. The man's voice was low. inarticulate, but presently he raised it, and Ross was able to catch some of the rapid French. A likely horse was running at Mandelieu next day and it seemed that the caller was anxious to place a bet. Just that.

Blackbeard brought Ross his *fine*.

"Here we do not joke about communists," he said defensively.

"Very wise of you." Ross nodded in the direction of a newspaper lying on one of the other tables. "Do you mind passing me that paper?"

Blackbeard hesitated. The calmness of the reply seemed to baffle him. Then, he shrugged and picked up the paper, a creased and battered copy of the current *Éclaireur*. He dropped it in front of Ross as if it were a challenge to a duel. Ross thanked him with a nod.

The young man at the phone finished his sporting conversation and spoke authoritatively across the zinc to the proprietor.

"Listen, Zizi, I am expecting my friend to call back. I'll have another glass while I'm waiting."

Zizi! The name was calamitously appropriate. Ross hid his grin behind the open sheet of the *Éclaireur*. The young man carried his wry neck to a table half way down the narrow room. A curious disability. Something paralysed. A war-wound perhaps. A scar running down from the left ear was faintly visible. The head was poised in an aquiline way, craning. The man could swivel it to the right but to look left he had to turn his body. He planted himself on the patched and napless plush of the *banquette* and leaned his head back against the grimy wall. That way he was squinting down his nose.

Ross read a story about the Countess Something-or-Other's party. He knew some of the names. The usual crowd. Mademoiselle Such-and-Such, the famous *vedette*, had strained a ligament in her calf. A couple of cars had collided on Californie, completely blocking the circulation for half an hour and gravely wounding Monsieur What's-His-Name, the well-known dentist.

Whenever he looked up and over the sheet, the slightly squinting eyes of the young man were on him. He turned more towards the door to avoid that inquisitive gaze. Margolies did not come, confound him! The brandy was terrible, the newspaper dull. Ross turned the sheet.

Flavius! The name leaped at him from the social notes.

Monsieur Vincent Flavius is spending the week-end at Juan-les-Pins. His trusted secretary and associate, the discreet but amiable Monsieur Caton Margolies, is returning to Cannes to-night to make arrangements for the further reception there of the distinguished American financier.

The door swung open. Ross moved abruptly, putting down the paper, but still there was no sign of the discreet, amiable Margolies. Instead, a young woman entered. A beautiful young woman. You noticed that at once. You also noticed that this was no social call and that she was desperately upset about something.

She hesitated on the threshold, but only for the fraction of time it took her to glance down the room. Then she ran forward, with the darting speed of a dancer, towards the man with the wry neck. There was a faint fresh fragrance in the disturbed air.

The young man rose and he was not pleased. He addressed her in a tone of alarmed protest, but she broke in on him violently. Her voice was low, subdued almost to a whisper, but the urgency was unmistakable. Ross caught her final words.

"You must come! Quickly!" She grasped the man's sleeve and tried to draw him towards the door. "Quickly!"

Trouble in the loose-box? Menace at Mandelieu?

The facetious questions flashed to his mind, but, before he could consider them, Ross saw that there was nothing to laugh at here. The young man pulled his sleeve away from her fingers, but she grasped at him again. This time he wrenched violently and caught hold of her.

"Sit down!" he commanded her, and went on inaudibly in an angry mutter.

Ross drank his *fine*. The customers farther down the room were too absorbed in their own boisterous argument to notice others. The waitress had retired to the kitchen. The bearded Zizi was caught up in some dull cloud of meditation from which he looked down at his zinc. Possibly the domestic (or extra-domestic) wrangle was a commonplace in his establishment. He began, meditatively, to pick his nose.

Damn the discreet but amiable Margolies!

Ross could hear the urgent voices still going on. He put his drink down.

As he did so, an odd thing happened. He stared straight into the eyes of the girl and she was looking at him as if she knew him. More, as if she were appealing to him. Then, wry-neck caught her roughly by one shoulder and slewed her round.

"Listen to me!" he demanded.

They were seated at the table now, the girl pleading, the man arguing. Ross watched them. Beauty and the Beast - but was it Beauty who was in distress this time, or the Beast? The question soon answered itself. Suddenly, she rose, as if she had made up her mind to some course. The man pulled her back to her seat.

Then the telephone rang and Zizi lumbered across the floor to pick up the receiver. Already the young man was on his feet.

"Wait!" he called to the girl. "Stay where you are!"

She got up but sat down again as if she had been cast back into indecision.

Zizi held out the receiver. "For you, monsieur."

Then things happened so quickly that Ross had no time for

anything but a blind obedience to impulse.

As her companion went to the telephone, the girl sprang up, jerking her chair back, and ran across the floor to Ross.

She spoke to him in English.

"Mr. Barnes, I must have your help. Come with me, quickly."

Ross stumbled confusedly to his feet.

She was saying: "Please, please! There may still be time."

In the background a sharp voice snapped out a word of agreement and the receiver went smack on to the hook. The man crossed from the telephone to the table in three quick strides. His right arm swung and his open hand caught the girl a vicious blow in the face and sent her towards the door.

"Hey, you . . . !" Ross began, but his left fist was out before his words. The man crashed against a table, recovered, and came back for more. He was a pitiable target with that out-thrust head on its twisted neck. Ross closed with him. He wanted an explanation, not a fight, but now he was trying to hold a clawing and kicking tiger. The man broke away and showered in blows. Ross jolted him and closed again. The girl was crying out to both of them to stop; but with wry-neck to deal with, it wasn't easy to stop.

They wrestled across the floor, overturning chairs, colliding with tables. Then the verbal brawlers from the end of the room intervened. Four arms pulled Ross away and held him, and his opponent wasted no time. He was free. Grasping the girl by one arm, he forced her to the door and out into the street.

The hands that had restrained Ross relaxed, and he started for the door. He knew now that the whole crazy incident must in some way be associated with Margolies, and that the girl held the secret of it. He must overtake her. The interveners laughed. Out in the street the fight might go on. They did not care. But Zizi stood in front of the door, a solid barrier.

"A hundred and fifty francs," he said.

Ross thrust a five-hundred note at him and made as if to pass.

"Wait!" Zizi was inexorable, an honest man. "I will give you your change."

He pulled a dirty change wallet from a pocket and began to count. By the time Ross reached the street it was too late. Light wind was blowing over Mont Chevalier. The shadow of the oleander moved on the wall. That was all.

Chapter 5

Striding down the narrow way towards the port, Ross was very angry.

He had had enough of these shennanigans. If Margolies wanted to play games, he could look for another stooge. And he could charter another craft. The man must be out of his mind; and Flavius himself could be little short of demented to employ such a lunatic.

Behind him on the hill the clock in the square tower of Notre Dame d'Espérance told him that it was nine, and nine was enough. If Margolies wanted him now, he could come to the jetty like any normal citizen. All this secrecy was positively infantile. In fact, the more he thought of the adventure, the more irrational and insane it seemed.

And yet . . . .

He halted suddenly. Supposing it wasn't irrational and insane? Supposing Margolies had been right to select a remote meeting-place like the *Café des Lauriers*? Supposing that there was a rational reason for this hitch in arrangements?

Ross turned and looked back up the steep street of the Suquet. He did not doubt that *Roselle* had been watched. It was now more than likely that the man with the bent neck had followed him from the corner of the Casino, trailing him to the café. But the girl could not have shadowed the man. She had appeared considerably later; and had come to the café with a purpose. It might be, then, that she was a messenger from Margolies.

Now that he thought of it, she had spoken English with a slight American intonation.

But she had gone straight to the man, as if that had been her purpose. Only later, in some sort of desperation, had she appealed to Ross.

It did not make sense. It was difficult to link up her behaviour with Margolies. But if she were not from Margolies, how could she have known the name of a complete stranger?

Ross went back to the café. Zizi came forward menacingly. "Now what?" he began. "Here we do not like . . ."

"All right, all right!" Ross slapped a hundred-franc note on the zinc. "I was waiting for a friend. He hasn't come. I just want to leave a message for him."

"We do not want your patronage!"

"You don't have to have it. Give me some paper and an envelope."

Zizi obeyed sulkily and pocketed the hundred francs. Resting a dog-eared tablet on the bar, Ross wrote a note to Margolies. He had, he said, waited an hour. He was now returning to the port. He scrawled the name of Monsieur Benj. Field on the envelope. The men from the back of the café had come forward to the proprietor's aid, eager, it seemed, to join in another fracas.

"Listen!" Ross said. "My name is Barnes. A man may come looking for me. An American, with long, thin fingers, like a pianist."

Zizi spat eloquently. He was anti-American, or he did not like music.

Ross shrugged and went. He had followed instructions and that was that. It was not in the charter that he should be involved in brawls in public places. He was still angry with Margolies as he went down the hill, and increasing pain from a barked shin did not improve his temper. He had been scratched as well as kicked, and now a demanding hunger was added to his woes. It grew with every limping step. It had to be satisfied, and it was going to be satisfied. If more waiting was to be done, Margolies could do it.

He went to a restaurant he knew in a side street off the Rue d'Antibes. He wished to be sure of friendly faces; to find an old friend, perhaps, or an acquaintance. He was disappointed to discover that the restaurant, like the café in the Suquet, was under new management. It had been enlarged and dolled up with indifferent murals, yet it had the old friendliness, and there were still stacks of baby langoustines in evidence. He could see no one he knew, but now he was too hungry to care.

When the first pangs were eased, he took everything in a leisurely way. This, in spite of the change, was Cannes, and he liked it. He no longer felt any rancour. He could contemplate Margolies losing some of his famous amiability with amusement. And as his own amiability increased, he looked back on the adventure of the *Café des Lauriers* with amusement. As an entertainment, it did not deserve to be classified as neo-Arabian, but there had been more than a touch of the Thousand and One Nights about it. And the lovely lady all forlorn had been quite up to standard. Lovely, in the best sense; not too glamorous and quite a bit dishevelled. Something of Mary about her; the eyes, perhaps. The vivid blueness was the same. Astonishing.

But the astonishing thing was that he could think of Mary without any more bitterness. He could see her point of view and he didn't blame her any longer. They had always taken things a bit lightly and he had been away so long, especially during the war, and that oaf she had married had had persuasive looks and a more persuasive bank account. That was life for you. Mary had a couple of kids with enlarged tonsils and he had *Roselle*. Compensation . . .

He looked at his supply of francs and ordered another half-carafe of *rosé*.

Of course, Eleanor was always nagging. Why didn't he take a wife and settle down? Because Mary had let him down, that didn't mean that all women were faithless.

But once was enough, wasn't it, even if the bitterness had gone? Nowadays he took an objective view of life, and it had its advantages. For instance, you could contemplate beauty in distress without immediately making a fatuously quixotic fool of yourself. You might, of course, throw a punch or two and take a kick on the shin, but . . .

He felt the honourable wound a little gingerly. It was easier for being rested.

Thank goodness for *Roselle*. Nothing faithless about her. Before

31

long, if things went well, he would have a small house to live in when he came ashore. He knew the spot he wanted. Outside Le Cannet, on the road to Grasse. He would have young Ralph down on occasions, and Eleanor and her husband could pay visits . . .

No end to it. No end.

He topped off an excellent meal with an Armagnac and a cigar. He felt fine, except that when he got up his shin was painful, but not painful enough to prevent his walking.

It was a lovely night, but dark, with a light wind blowing from the Estérel. There was no moon and the stars shone only mistily through a thin overcast.

He hurried, feeling a little guilty. If Margolies had really gone to the jetty, he had been kept waiting long enough. And there were Ralph and Tiny Kane. They were due for a turn ashore. They should have it, too. One thing he had made up his mind on. He was not going to sail till morning, no matter what Margolies or Flavius might have to say.

There were lights in the yachts that made up the long close row along the pier. Radios were going in some of them, and in one it seemed that a party was in progress. Ross hummed a tune that he heard as he passed. Twenty yards farther along he stopped humming and stood rigid on the paved edge of the jetty, staring at a dark slot of water between two of the larger cabin cruisers.

Roselle was gone.

Chapter 6

It was near eleven, he told the police, when he made the discovery. He could not say how near, because he had been too flabbergasted at that moment to think of looking at his watch. The hour that then concerned him was the hour of *Roselle*'s departure from the jetty.

But of course he had made inquiries. No one had been able to give him specific information. The few men on the nearby craft had been half asleep or indifferent. The *Liberté* might sail from that pier without being noticed. All he had learned was that engine sounds had been heard about nine o'clock. That statement was from a seaman on the schooner with the dark hull.

"He was on deck soon after nine and saw then that *Roselle* had sailed," Ross added.

The inspector nodded blandly. He was a mild-mannered man with a thin, greying thatch on a round head. "The question now, monsieur," he said, "is what can I do for you?"

Ross stared at him.

"Can't you send out an alarm? To the coastguards or your navy patrols. Surely something can be done. I want my vessel back. No one had the right to take her out without my permission."

Ross was angry again, as angry as he had been when he had run from the jetty shouting for a taxi to take him to the police commissioner. He wasn't going to be treated like this by any Flavius or Margolies. Not for all the money in the Federal Reserve and the Bank of England combined. It was robbery, piracy!

The inspector was very calm. "We must look at the situation from all sides, Monsieur Barnes. You say you were quite prepared to sail to-night on the instruction of your friends?"

"I did not say friends. I was prepared to sail with myself in charge. I went to the café in the Suquet to discuss arrangements."

"And you left a deputy in command of your yacht."

"Not with authority to sail."

"You gave him that direction in so many words?"

"He understood perfectly that he was not to move till I returned."

"He understood?" The inspector looked up at the ceiling, then down at his desk. "You mean that that was your understanding. The fact is that this Monsieur Flavius is the charterer of your vessel."

"It is established by the charter party that I, as owner, remain in charge."

"Under the orders of the charterer though, surely?"

"Monsieur!" Ross hauled his chair closer to the desk. "No one had a right to give sailing orders over my head. And my man Kane would not have accepted such orders."

The inspector spread out his hands persuasively. "Perhaps Monsieur Flavius merely wished to test the vessel. A little tour round the Lérins. Perhaps by now the *Roselle* is back in her berth. It is impossible to imagine that a great man like Monsieur Flavius could possibly engage in anything incorrect."

Ross let out a breath he had been holding. "I don't even know that Flavius is engaged in this thing at all. I don't know what to think. That letter I've given you. How do I know it really came from Margolies? It may be a forgery, a fake."

"Ah, but we must be serious." The inspector looked reproachful. "Who could have known that a letter was to be directed to you at Marseilles?"

"I can't say. All I know is that the café business was a trick, to get me out of the way. I was watched and followed. The man with the bent neck talked about a horse on the telephone. That was another trick. The horse at Mandelieu meant that I was at the *Café des Lauriers*. The return telephone call was to tell the fellow that the yacht had sailed."

"And the young lady – the beautiful young lady – she suddenly decided to betray everything?" The inspector smiled, shaking his head.

Ross gestured angrily, bringing a fist down on his knee.

The inspector became paternal.

"I agree, monsieur, that it must have seemed mysterious. Yet you were not alarmed at the time. You walked from this café, you took your time over dinner, and it is in fact nearly eleven when you return to the *Jetée Albert-Édouard*. And then, monsieur! Then you put this new construction on the incidents. Then you see everything in a sinister light. Possibly Monsieur Margolies was prevented from going to the café in time and hoped to see you on the jetty."

Ross exploded. "But surely you can do something? There's a boy on that yacht, a young nephew of mine. I am responsible, you understand? If anything happens to him . . ."

"I understand your anxiety, Monsieur." The inspector was avuncular now. "But I think it is a little too early to give way to panic. Perhaps if we could satisfy you that your charterer is really on board the yacht you will feel easier."

"And if you could satisfy yourself that he isn't on board?" Ross snatched at the hope of getting some action. "According to the newspaper, Flavius is in Juan-les-Pins for the weekend."

"Sometimes stories are circulated for the convenience of Monsieur Flavius. He has been staying in Nice. That much I know. We have to keep an eye on our distinguished visitors. One moment, Monsieur Barnes, while I make an inquiry."

Ross was left alone in the small bleak office with nothing to do but stare at a faded bromide enlargement in a heavy frame. There were a lot of policemen on an annual picnic. Or it may have been a man-hunt. One of them, no doubt, was the inspector when younger and perhaps less complacent.

The inspector returned. "Yes," he said. "At least we have definite news of your friend Margolies. He arrived from Nice this evening and went to the *Marinville* where a suite is being reserved for the Flavius party." The inspector picked up his telephone. "We will see what happens."

He asked for the *Marinville* and waited. He asked for Monsieur

Margolies and waited again. The pause seemed endless to Ross, When the inspector spoke again, he was very brief. "Oui!" he said. "Entendu." Then he put down the receiver.

"It is just as I thought," he announced. "Monsieur Margolies left the hotel at eight o'clock and has not yet returned."

Ross stared.

"Perhaps," the inspector added with an encouraging smile, "he induced your engineer to run along the coast to pick up Monsieur Flavius. I am sure that everything will be explained in the morning."

"Do you mean that you are going to do nothing until the morning?"

"Our men on night duty at the port will be ordered to keep a specially sharp look-out. As soon as there is news, I will communicate with you. Where will you be staying?"

Ross had not had time to realise that he was stranded, with nothing more than he stood up in. "I'll probably get a room at the *Parc*," he said. "If not, I'll telephone you."

"Excellent! Guizet. Inspector Guizet. I hope we shall find that your fears were groundless."

He bestowed a grave smile - the good-natured doctor gently dismissing a confirmed hypochondriac.

Ross booked a room at the *Parc*, then telephoned the *Marinville*. He learned that Margolies was still absent. The information served, illogically, to increase his anxiety. He went back down to the port, only to find the same dark gap in the row of pleasure craft. He walked out to the seaward end of the jetty and stood staring across the water at the light on the breakwater.

When he turned he could see the eyes of the girl in the *Café des Lauriers* and they were full of desperation. He heard urgency in her voice. He thought of Ralph and Kane and for the hundredth time wondered where they were and what was happening to them.

Perhaps Guizet was right, and he was making a melodrama out of a misunderstanding. Perhaps the girl had merely wanted to tell him that Margolies had gone straight to *Roselle* and he, Ross, should return to the yacht before it was too late.

Too late to sail?

One thought after another buzzed in his head. He hurried away from the jetty. He walked along the Croisette, then back again. The black water in which *Roselle* had berthed was as still as a lake.

He was tired. His mind could no longer grapple with the problem. He returned to his hotel and got into bed.

Some time in the night, after hours of staring into the frightened eyes of the girl in the café, he fell asleep. The next thing he knew there was grey light at the window and someone was banging on the door.

Guizet was bundled up in a tight raincoat with a belt round the middle. He looked as grey and haggard as the dawn itself.

He didn't say good morning. He said: "You carried a white-painted dinghy on your yacht, monsieur?"

Ross was awake. "You have some news?"

"Of a kind. You had better put your clothes on and come with me."

"What do you mean, for God's sake?" Ross felt his stomach dropping away from him.

The inspector answered. "A dinghy has been found. There is someone in it - a man. We do not know him. We wish you to identify him, if you can."

"Do you mean he's dead?"

"Yes. It would seem that he has been murdered. I have a car waiting downstairs. If you will dress quickly, we can be there soon."

They sped out of the town by the Rue d'Antibes and struck the coast road the other side of the Cap de la Croisette. Ross thought their destination would be Juan-les-Pins, but the driver came to a stop a little to the east of Golfe-Juan.

The dinghy was drawn up on the beach, and small waves came in from a grey sea to lap against the stern.

Two men in uniform guarded the find and three others waited, drawn a little apart. The three were local fishermen. They had come across the drifting boat; beached it and reported their discovery. There was no one else about. Golfe-Juan was still asleep. The two groups by the dinghy looked like mourners at a graveside divided by some old family quarrel.

A borrowed tarpaulin had been thrown across the dinghy to hide its contents. One of the uniformed men pulled it away as Guizet and Ross plodded across the sand.

Ross was prepared. The inspector had been able to furnish a description that disposed at least of the fear that it might be Ralph. The tattooing on the left forearm would have been enough. Quite enough. Bewilderment and the anger that had supervened had kept Ross silent on the ride. Now, as he came to the side of the dinghy, he was filled with horror and dread.

The body was tumbled clumsily across the thwarts with knees drawn up, with the head in the bows and the dead face turned to the sky. It looked as if the man had collapsed while rowing. One oar was still held by the port rowlock. The other was missing.

Guizet waited before asking the inevitable question.

"Yes," Ross said. "It is Kane."

He could add no word to that at the moment. He did not want to see any more, but he had to look at everything. All the details. Tiny's shirt was a mess of blood from a bullet wound in the body, and blood from another wound in the head had drawn dark distorting lines down his face.

"The full name, if you please, monsieur?"

"Kane," Ross answered automatically. "Edward John Kane."

Chapter 7

A doctor, a police photographer, and some other sort of expert arrived from Cannes. Guizet greeted them briefly, but ignored their activities. He spoke to the fishermen. He squinted at his watch, then glanced along the curving stretch of the Antibes road beyond the railway line. He frowned. He looked rumpled, ill-groomed, as if some impatient hand had tossed him into his clothes and crammed a hat down on his head before he could reach his greying hair with a comb. But his manner was still mild. Again and again he glanced along the road, and at last he was rewarded by the sight of a car speeding from the direction of Juan-les-Pins.

He spoke to the stunned Ross Barnes and his tone was paternal again.

"Monsieur, you had better come with me."

The car was another police vehicle. A tall man disengaged himself from the front seat and hurried to meet Guizet.

"It is true," he told the inspector. "They are all there at the *Hotel Alexandre*. The visit was arranged by Merle-Florac."

"They are all there?"

"All. Typist, valet, chauffeur."

"And Monsieur Flavius himself?"

"Apparently. None of them is yet out of bed."

"You saw the night clerk?"

"Yes. The valet left word that his master was not to be disturbed."

"We will change it." For a moment Guizet looked a little grim.

Ross listened, trying to make sense of the words. The tall plain-clothes man was young. He had uncertain eyes in a handsome, rather heavy face. He was excited. He kept fumbling at the buttons of his jacket.

"Merle-Florac?" Guizet repeated speculatively.

"He is the big industrialist from the north."

"Yes."

"That is why the American makes this visit to Juan-les-Pins. It is understandable. It is business. The *Alexandre* is a suitable place, exclusive, discreet."

"Remarkable!"

The sarcasm had no bite. It was a gentle reproach. The tall man went on unperturbed.

"Reservations for Merle-Florac were made in the name of Moreau. There is, possibly, some big business on foot."

"The night clerk talks freely."

"He is my brother-in-law."

"Then we can keep it in the family. The business I am interested in is murder. We will take your car. You will stay here and learn what the doctor has to say." Guizet turned to Ross and urged him into motion with pressure on his arm. "You and I, Monsieur Barnes, will have some questions for your charterer."

Ross turned. His numbed senses were beginning to work again. "What can Flavius know?" he said. "If he's ashore, he's out of it. The question is : where is *Roselle* and my young nephew? What are you doing to find them?"

"Everything," Guizet answered quietly. "The naval authorities have been alerted. An alarm has been sent out to all shipping in the vicinity. As soon as a sighting report is received, we shall have it."

"Sighting report! The boy's in the hands of murderers. He's only a youngster. He can't look after himself. Something's got to be done. Something . . . It's Margolies at the back of it all. Can't you see that? He had it all worked out from the beginning. He's up to some game of his own. Who cares about Flavius? It's the boy I'm worrying about."

"Get into the car, Monsieur Barnes."

The voice was mild, but the pressure on the elbow was firm.

"I understand how you feel," the inspector murmured. "But you must be calm. We cannot swim out into the sea after your ship. We are two small people. We have forces behind us, but first we must know what we are dealing with. Until then, calm."

The voice was different when he addressed the desk clerk in the sumptuous foyer of the *Alexandre*.

"I am Inspector Guizet. I wish to speak to Monsieur Flavius at once."

The clerk protested that he could not disturb a guest. The inspector raised his voice. It echoed harshly in the marble recesses of the still deserted lobby.

"Monsieur Flavius himself," the voice demanded. "No servants. Telephone to his room. It is urgent."

"Monsieur . . ."

"At once!"

The clerk manipulated the switchboard and rang. He waited a moment and rang again. He rang a third time.

"There is no reply," he said.

The mild-mannered Guizet whirled into action as if someone had fired a starting pistol.

"Quickly!" He snapped his fingers to command service from a page-boy. "The number of the suite? The key! A house key!" He was on his way to the lift, dragging Ross along and driving the page-boy before him. Up they shot and along a wide corridor they hurried, wading through the thick pile of the carpet.

The page-boy pointed to a door and Guizet hammered on it. He shouted and hammered again. Then he tried the handle, but there was a spring lock on the door and the handle turned nothing. He used the key, threw the door open wide and entered the living-room.

There was nobody there. In the bedroom and bathroom beyond were the contents of an overnight suitcase, but the bed had not been slept in. In the living-room there was nothing to show that Vincent J. Flavius had ever been there except a spent match and a half-smoked cigar in an ashtray.

A protesting valet in shirt-sleeves had already arrived in the living-room, and in a moment he was joined by a sleek young woman who looked vaguely incomplete without a shorthand notebook. She contrived to appear both haughty and bewildered at the same time when Guizet introduced himself. The clerk must have been busy at the switchboard, for a moment later the chauffeur also arrived.

"Is this the whole entourage?" Guizet wanted to know.

"Except for Caton," the stenographer answered.

"That is Mr. Margolies," the valet explained. "He went on ahead of us to Cannes."

Timing everything very, very nicely, Ross thought bitterly, and he could no longer stand by in silence.

"What was he going to do with the yacht when he'd stolen it?" he demanded in English.

Three heads turned and three pairs of eyes stared at him in amazement.

"Silence!" snapped Guizet. "I am the one who will ask the questions. For the moment, Monsieur Barnes, you will listen."

The three heads turned again as if worked by one piece of mechanism. Amazement in the eyes was deeper, if anything, and now the chauffeur was unable to restrain himself.

"What the hell is all this?" he said. "Where's the chief? What's happened?" His English was strongly accented, but with American intonations.

The inspector ordered him to speak French. Ross began to translate, but the chauffeur supplied his own interpretation, with trimmings. The stenographer and valet, too, became voluble and urgent, and it was some time before Guizet could extract any facts.

At first they were all sure that the chief must be somewhere in the hotel, perhaps in the suite of Monsieur Merle-Florac, but a telephone inquiry, carefully phrased so as to be quite uninformative, brought the news that he was not.

Guizet concentrated on the stenographer, first writing down her name as if he were about to take a formal deposition. She was Madeleine Blieke and she came from Milwaukee, Wisconsin. She admitted twenty-seven years, the last six of which she had spent in the employment of Mr. Flavius.

"Delbert drove us over from Nice yesterday afternoon," she said. "We arrived about five."

Delbert confirmed it.

"You all travelled in the same car?" Guizet inquired.

Miss Blieke nodded. "The four of us. In the Rolls. Caton left in the morning in the Cadillac."

"No, no," Delbert objected. "Caton took the Jaguar. I left the Cadillac in the garage at Nice."

The valet explained : "The Jaguar is Caton's own car."

"First I will listen to Mademoiselle Blieke," Guizet asserted.

It was not easy. The others would keep butting in. It was established by argument, for instance, that the valet, Frederick Schuper, had the latest knowledge of the chief, but the sum of all the evidence was very little.

Mr. Flavius had had a busy day, and by the time he had got to the *Alexandre*, he had been tired. He had bathed and put on a dark blue suit, then dictated a cable to America and one or two unimportant letters. Later he had gone to the suite of Merle-Florac for cocktails. He had returned to his own suite and eaten a modest dinner there. He was on a diet, and liked to eat early. The chauffeur had not seen him after he had entered the hotel and Miss Blieke had been dismissed before his visit to Merle-Florac, but the valet had spoken to him after dinner in that very room and had received instructions about pressing some clothes. At the time, about eight-thirty, Schuper estimated, Mr. Flavius was sitting in an armchair, smoking a cigar.

"He told me he was expecting a call from Caton," the valet said. "After that, he was going to bed. I don't know if he received the call from Caton."

It was always Caton, never Margolies. The familiarity had a curious kind of reverence in it, as if they all looked upon the secretary as a big brother who would never let them down.

"Perhaps the chief changed his mind and went on to Cannes last night?" Miss Blieke suggested.

"Without letting you know? Without calling for his car?" inquired the inspector.

"He has sometimes done that sort of thing, when he has wanted to avoid people. In any case, I had better phone through to the *Marinville* and speak to Caton."

"No!" The inspector's monosyllable was very sharp. "I will do the speaking, and first I will speak with Monsieur Merle-Florac. Meanwhile you three will remain within the hotel."

He motioned to Ross to accompany him to the suite of the great man from the north.

There was a slight delay. The personal secretary informed the inspector that the great man was seeing nobody.

"You are deceived," Guizet observed in his mildest manner. "He is seeing me. You will be good enough to inform him at once that Monsieur Flavius was kidnapped from this hotel last night. At once, if you please."

Chapter 8

Jean-Louis Merle-Florac, the big industrialist from the north, was a small man, and the voluminous brocade dressing-gown he wore over his massive silk pyjamas seemed to emphasise the fact. He came of the nobility. His parents, now departed, had always insisted on the ancient style of address. They had been the Comte and Comtesse de Merle-Florac, but, to Jean-Louis, machine tools were more than titles and he had dropped what he had come to regard as an absurdity. He derived his authority not from the vanished lands of his ancestors, but from his directorships, his shares in holding companies, his position in a cartel. He had rejected with contemptuous amusement the proposal of an estate agent that he should buy back the ancient chateau of Merle-Florac. What would he want with that antiquated fossil of a place? A sensible man lived in apartments and hotels. They were flexible, they were convenient, they could be changed at a whim. And the roofs never leaked.

Or did they, sometimes?

Monsieur Merle-Florac seemed to be afflicted by a doubt as he came from his bedroom. His slippers had his initials embroidered in gold on the toe-caps and they seemed to peep tentatively at the world outside the pyjamas. As tentatively as his eyes peered from their puffy recesses. They were like two dry currants embedded in putty. He might have been cast, without make-up, for something disagreeable in Molière. Undeniably disagreeable; and also, possibly, dangerous.

"What is this nonsense?" He stared at the top button of Guizet's waistcoat. "Flavius has an appointment with me for eleven o'clock this morning."

"Nevertheless, monsieur . . ."

"We are to discuss important business matters!" The small eyes rose to the left lapel of the inspector's jacket. "Why should he be missing?"

"That is for me to discover." Guizet kept his gaze quite steady. "Monsieur Flavius has disappeared, a yacht has been stolen from the port of Cannes, a murder has been committed . . ."

Merle-Florac dismissed it all with an impatient gesture. "I am a business man, Inspector. I am not interested in melodrama. If he has not . . ." He broke off uncertainly. The penny had dropped. "What did you say?" he demanded. "A murder?"

Possibly the shock of it made him look straight at them. It was a glance, immediately withdrawn, but in the fraction of a second Ross thought he saw fear in the man's eyes.

Briefly, Guizet told the story of the charter of *Roselle* and then of the discovery on the beach at Golfe-Juan. Monsieur Merle-Florac sat down rather suddenly, his face the colour of chalk. It seemed that he had a nervous heart. It was caused by overwork, he explained. Talk of death and violence always upset him. He sat for a moment or two in silence, his eyes closed. The recovery, when it came, was as sudden as the collapse. He opened his eyes.

"This is mere coincidence," he snapped. "I know too well the chi-chi our American friend likes to make. If he has disappeared it is in order to create an impression, a show."

"Perhaps it is a coincidence that Margolies chartered my craft?" Ross interposed.

"Margolies?" The suggestion made Merle-Florac smirk. "You think that Margolies, the trusted lieutenant, is a traitor? No, no! It is all in the pattern. Flavius the Great! The unpredictable prima donna of the stock market! Now he is here, now he is gone! This business of the chartered vessel is just part of a publicity game. Any fool can see that."

"But I, monsieur," Guizet remarked quietly; "I can also see the corpse in the boat."

"I assure you I am not the assassin."

"It was never in my mind that you could be."

"Then why do you come here? What can I do?"

"Monsieur Flavius came to this place to meet you. I wish to know what passed between you."

"Nothing but a few friendly words. We had a cocktail. He was supposed to dine with me and to talk business. He excused himself. He felt very tired, he said. He must leave our business until the morning. In any case, he must wait until he heard from Margolies in Cannes. He did not explain why he had to hear from Margolies."

"You did not ask him?"

"Why should I? He would not have told me the truth."

Inspector Guizet blinked as if an illusion had been shattered.

"What was this important business you were to discuss?" he inquired.

Merle-Florac frowned. Clearly, the question was in bad taste. "Surely you do not expect me to tell you that?" he said irritably.

"There have been rumours of some sort of merger," the inspector persisted.

Merle-Florac looked out of the window. He was very intent on the Mediterranean, even though there was no sail on the sea to engage his attention. "Wherever Flavius goes," he said, "there are rumours of mergers. Nothing I could tell you would be of any help to the police."

"The police will certainly wish to form their own opinion about that, monsieur." The inspector's cheeks were slightly pink now.

"Yes?" Monsieur did not turn his head. "I will tell my friend, the Minister of Justice, what you say. No doubt he will consult with you on the point."

The inspector was silent for a moment. Ross saw the pink spread to his neck and ears. When next he spoke, however, his voice was quiet and level.

"Then you have no reason for believing that this disappearance is in any way abnormal?" he said.

Merle-Florac turned impatiently. "You are a detective. Do not the facts convey anything to you? Margolies hires this Englishman's yacht." He motioned with a jerk of his head towards Ross. "The very night the vessel arrives in Cannes, Flavius slips away from this hotel and presently both Flavius and the yacht are missing. If you think that is extraordinary you should consult Margolies, not me."

"Monsieur Margolies left the *Hotel Marinville* between seven and eight last night, saying that he was dining out. He has not yet returned."

"Then he is probably with Flavius. And now if I can be of no further service to you. . . ."

They were dismissed. The inspector sighed faintly.

"May I ask how long you intend to stay in Juan-les-Pins, monsieur?" he said.

"Just so long as it suits me."

"It may be necessary for me to see you again."

"I assure you it will be quite unnecessary. Certainly, I cannot undertake to remain here for your convenience. In any case, you will know where to find me. I am not unknown in France."

"As you say, monsieur." Guizet brought his heels together with the faintest of clicks and inclined slightly towards the shrivelled mandarin.

Outside in the corridor, he stared at the closed door of the suite for a moment, but he gave Ross no inkling of what was in his mind. When he moved, it was with an abrupt gesture. "We will go downstairs," he said.

Chapter 9

For Ross, every moment away from the sight of the sea was a moment wasted. *Roselle* was somewhere out there. Perhaps she had been found. Perhaps she was being brought back to port. His impatience had become intolerable. He wanted to be watching the horizon for the first sign of the craft, to know whether she was alive or derelict, but the inspector kept him at his side, and the inspector was busy in the spacious lobby of the palms and marble columns, or in the small but comfortably furnished office of the manager. In one place or the other he questioned all members of the staff who had been on duty from the time of the arrival of the Flavius party until midnight.

At first the information that emerged seemed desultory and quite useless. Guizet was particularly interested in telephone calls, but none had come in after eight-thirty, the time of the valet's dismissal for the night. In spite of the paragraph in the *Éclaireur*, little popular notice had been taken of the great man's arrival in Juan-les-Pins. Only one call from outside had been recorded, and that was from a newspaper man some time before seven. "Mademoiselle Blieke took the message," the operator said. Otherwise the telephone had been used only for exchanges with the Merle-Florac suite.

The inspector made notes. The book he used was very small, but Ross reflected that it was more than adequate. He had the temerity, at last, to utter a protest.

"Couldn't these routine inquiries come later?" he said. "I feel we ought to go to the *Café des Lauriers*? I'm convinced that that fellow with the twisted neck knew something."

The inspector ignored him blandly and proceeded to question the concierge who had been on duty in the lobby all the evening. Mademoiselle Blieke, they learned, had gone out alone about seven o'clock, but had returned for dinner at nine-fifteen. The chauffeur, too, had left the hotel about seven. He had consulted the doorman about a place where he could eat well. The chauffeur had returned about midnight. The concierge had seen nothing of the valet, Monsieur Schuper. And nothing of Monsieur Flavius; but a man had arrived with a message. That must have been soon after eight-thirty. He had given it to Roger to take up to the suite. The man had not waited for an answer.

"What sort of man?" Guizet inquired. "Describe him, if you please."

The concierge shook his head. "What sort? A messenger. So many come and go. I was occupied at the time with other things, and he did not wait."

"No local man? No one you knew?"

"If I had known him, I would have remembered him," the concierge said simply.

Roger, a diminutive page-boy about fifteen, remembered carrying the message. The envelope was blue; the address scrawled in pencil. He had knocked on the door and Monsieur Flavius himself had called to him to enter. Monsieur had got up from a chair, put down a half-smoked cigar, read the message and pushed it into a pocket of his jacket.

That half-smoked cigar in the ashtray!

"What else?" the inspector demanded,

"What more?" Roger countered. "He said there was no reply and I could go. That, at least, I understood. His French is difficult."

"Was he worried when he read the message? Did he frown? Did he show any feeling?"

"He was pleased. He laughed. I thought . . . But it is not evidence, what I thought."

"Never mind. We will examine it." The inspector gazed benignly on this shrimp with a feeling for the rules of evidence. "What did you think?"

The shrimp leered. "I thought there was a woman mixed up in it," he said.

Guizet stared at the boy as though his confidence had been betrayed.

"You think this pencil scrawl was in a woman's hand?"

Roger shook his head. "I did not study it."

"Perhaps, then, you were near enough to Monsieur Flavius to study the letter?"

"No. I saw only that it was on blue paper."

"In that case, why do you say there was a woman mixed up in it?"

"There always is." Roger grinned and made a suggestive sound with his lips.

Guizet looked annoyed. "That's enough of that, my lad," he said sharply.

"You asked me what I thought," Roger complained stoutly. "I told you it was not evidence."

Guizet sighed. "Let us return to Monsieur Flavius, if you please. He told you there was no reply and you could go?"

"That is what I understood him to say. He was not so grammatical."

"This was shortly after eight-thirty? You left the suite and you did not see him any more?"

"No, monsieur. I saw him a few minutes later, in the foyer."

"Downstairs?"

"Assuredly downstairs. I held the door for him and he went out. He gave me a dollar bill and said something in English. I think it was that he wished me to buy a hotel for myself. He was still very pleased, so you see . . ."

"No more of your thoughts," Guizet interrupted quickly. "The concierge says he saw nothing of Monsieur Flavius in the foyer."

"At that moment Henri was attending to something in the baggage-room. Monsieur Carrel was busy at the desk. It was the dinner-hour and the foyer was empty of guests. Monsieur Flavius did not use the lift. Perhaps he wished to depart unobserved."

"How was he dressed?"

"In a dark blue suit. No hat. No coat. I think, therefore, he meant to return. I went out on to the front terrace to see who was meeting him, but there was no one in sight. At the end of the drive, he took the turning towards the sea. And that was truly the last I saw of him. If he meant to go off with a woman, it is strange that he did not wear a hat. He is quite bald."

"An unfortunate condition!" Guizet's mouth twitched a little. "I am grateful to you, my little one."

"It is nothing." Roger's world-weary shrug dismissed the matter. "There is one other thing," he added casually. "I remained on the terrace, and some time later Mademoiselle Blieke came hurrying from the direction of the sea. She looked a little strange."

Guizet jerked himself up in his chair. "How is that? Strange?"

"Worried, perhaps. She was out of breath, as if she had been running."

"She was late for dinner, perhaps?"

"Late? How could she be late? The restaurant is open all the evening. Mademoiselle Fournaise came in quite fifteen minutes after Mademoiselle Blieke."

"Who is Mademoiselle Fournaise?"

"She is of the Merle-Florac party; the assistant to the personal secretary."

Inspector Guizet decided to give further attention to the Flavius stenographer, but he did not go up again to the suite. Having dismissed Roger, he telephoned to Miss Blieke and asked her to come down to the manager's office.

She came promptly, though somewhat irritably, and this time Ross took more notice of her. She had red hair of a fiery tint, but this was the only vivid note contributed by nature, for the shade of lipstick she used seemed to emphasise rather than mitigate the pallor of her complexion. The eyes were a washed-out blue. Behind their mask of irritation, they looked scared.

Guizet was mildly apologetic.

"One or two small inquiries, Mademoiselle," he said. "I understand that you received a telephone call from a newspaper correspondent."

"Yes." The monosyllable came eagerly, as if she were suddenly relieved.

The inspector waited and his silence disconcerted her.

"They are always asking for interviews," she went on, after a moment. "I have authority to deal with them. Mr. Flavius will never grant interviews to individual reporters."

"Who was the man?"

"He was from the Herald-Tribune. The Paris office, of course."

"His name?"

"I did not ask."

"You are sure he was from the Herald-Tribune?"

"I only know what he told me. He was telephoning from Cannes, that I do know. I heard the operator. He said he had been assigned to talk to Monsieur Flavius. I told him it was quite out of the question. There was nothing unusual about that. You don't think . . .?"

She left the question in the air.

Guizet said: "Do you know that a note was delivered to Monsieur Flavius about eight-thirty last night; that a few minutes later he walked from this hotel?"

She was rigid and silent, as if incapable of movement or speech. At last she shook her head.

"No, I didn't know that," she said.

"Where were you at the time?"

"In the restaurant."

Now the inspector paused. He got up from his chair, walked across the room and looked at a calendar that hung beside the door. Miss Blieke raised a pale hand to her red hair. The inspector was studying a highly-coloured picture of the Gorges du Loup on the calendar. He turned slowly, to put his next question.

"You saw nothing of this message, this note, mademoiselle? On blue paper?"

"I left Monsieur Flavius before he went to see Merle-Florac." The girl still fingered her hair.

"But this morning?" The inspector was gentle in his insistence. "He might have thrown it down, in the wastebasket."

"No."

"You are sure?"

"Yes. There was nothing in the room."

"Then you searched? You looked in the waste-basket, for instance?"

But Roger, the page-boy, had stated clearly that Flavius had pushed the note into his pocket. Ross was about to remind the inspector, but a swift gesture halted him. Miss Blieke's face was a shade or two paler.

"After you questioned us, monsieur," she said quickly. "Naturally I was anxious to see . . ."

"You suspected?"

"I wanted to help."

"You saw that I was neglectful? That was clever. You realised that some important clue might be there in the suite, waiting to be found?"

"That is what I thought."

"Then you realised that in some way your employer had been induced to leave the hotel?"

"There had to be some explanation."

"Exactly." The inspector was sympathetic. "At what hour did you come down to dinner, mademoiselle?"

If he intended a trap, Miss Blieke was wary. She said: "It was about eight-thirty when I went into the restaurant, I think."

"You think . . ." The inspector was again absorbed by the Gorges du Loup. From the nodding motion of his head he seemed to be counting every arch in the viaduct that straddled the collotype landscape.

"So . . ." he murmured, and then turned to face her once more, "And between seven and eight-thirty?"

"I went for a walk."

"Yes?" He cleared his throat. "The concierge makes it nine-fifteen when you returned. A page-boy who saw you hurrying from the direction of the sea testifies that it was considerably after eight-thirty. They may be mistaken, since you say you went in to dine at eight-thirty?"

Miss Blieke moistened her lips with her tongue. Knuckles rapped on the door and the manager came apologetically into his own sanctum.

"Pardon, Inspector, there is a telegram for . . ."

"Wait!" Guizet snapped harshly. His voice softened again surprisingly as he returned to Miss Blieke. "Mademoiselle, if you please?"

"The mistake, no doubt, is mine," Miss Blieke said. "I had no reason to pay much attention to the time."

"But you were hurrying, I believe? One hurries when time is a consideration."

"I knew it was getting on. I did not want to be late for dinner." She moistened her lips again. "I was hungry."

"Of course. The little promenade had given you an appetite. You were walking all the two hours?"

"No. I stopped to rest."

The thwarted manager saw his opportunity in a pause. He stepped forward from the doorway, flourishing the telegram.

"It is for Monsieur Flavius," he announced protestingly. "It must . . ."

The words died on his lips as Guizet glared at him balefully. There was a brief silence. "Attend, mademoiselle! Where did you go on this promenade?"

"To the shore and along by the sea."

"By which route to the shore?"

"I crossed the railway at the station. I don't see how it can interest you. I suppose I spent some time looking in shops."

"You went into some of the shops?"

"I bought some nougat and I stopped at a bar for a cassis."

"Which bar?"

"I did not notice any name. It faced the sea."

"You have been here with Monsieur Flavius before? You are familiar with Juan-les-Pins?"

"Yes."

"Thank you, mademoiselle." Guizet turned to the fuming manager. "Now, if you please, the telegram."

The man's view of the inspector was expressed in a look. Miss Blieke took the telegram from him, slit the seal, and flicked the sheet open expertly. She frowned as she read the contents, then handed the sheet to the inspector with a shrug.

Guizet frowned in his turn. "What does it mean?" he demanded. "Who is Aristotle? Who is Sophocles?"

"I don't know," Miss Blieke answered. "Caton and Monsieur Flavius have code names for people."

"So I gather. Well?"

"There are sometimes highly confidential negotiations and I am informed only when they are completed."

"One of these names could refer to Merle-Florac?"

Miss Blieke hesitated. "I am merely the personal stenographer," she answered.

"But that is surely a position of trust?"

"Exactly." A note of cold determination came into her voice. "I am trusted not to make guesses about things that do not concern me."

Guizet shrugged, and passed the telegram to Ross. "Here, Monsieur Barnes," he said, "is something from your friend Margolies. Possibly you will see in it an explanation of why he did not meet you at the *Café des Lauriers* last night."

The message had been handed in at Marseilles that morning. It read:

OBLIGED TO MOTOR ON HERE LAST NIGHT CONSEQUENCE
WORD FROM SOPHOCLES WAITING AT CANNES STOP HOPE
IRON OUT HITCH THIS MORNING STOP SUGGEST YOU POSTPONE
FINAL CLINCH ARISTOTLE PENDING RESULT OPERATION
BOUILLABAISSE STOP HOPE REACH CANNES BY NINE TONIGHT
LATEST - CATON

Chapter 10

The inspector and Ross drove back to Cannes.

Ross was both puzzled by the telegram and deeply suspicious of it. The message was so unlike the supposed author of it. Margolies would never think of applying to negotiations in Marseilles such a facetious term as Operation Bouillabaisse. Those long, slender pianistic fingers of his would describe a turn of horror at the mere suggestion, the Harvard nose would wrinkle, the lofty brow knit in an expression of elegant disdain. The telegram must be a trick intended to start a false scent in Marseilles.

Guizet listened absently as Ross put the point, but made no positive comment on it. He seemed to be thinking of other things.

"I am not at all sure about that young woman with the red hair," he remarked after a while. "I don't think she was telling the truth about that little promenade."

"What we have to do is find the woman with the dark hair," Ross said. "A complete stranger, yet she called me by name!"

"She bought nougat and had a cassis."

"I am talking about the woman in the *Café des Lauriers*."

"I will find out where she bought the nougat. I will examine the waiter who brought her the cassis. I will trace every step of her little promenade."

"Do you intend to examine the patron of the *Lauriers*?" Ross demanded.

"Eh?" The inspector turned to gaze at him. "Oh, yes. We are on the way there, my friend. Oh, yes."

The ponderous, black-bearded proprietor nodded gloomily when the inspector identified himself. Clearly, he had had dealings with the police before.

"You are Pierre Masson?" the inspector inquired mildly.

"I am Pierre Masson. So what would you? I told your spy last night that there are no communists here. None!"

"That is interesting, but not pertinent," the inspector observed gravely. "For all I care you can have Marx and Engels upstairs and Molotov under the zinc. I desire to know about two customers who were here last night."

"Possibly your spy knows more than I do, since he interfered with them and made a rough-house. To me they were strangers. I never saw them before."

Ross interposed. "The man knew you. He called you Zizi."

"Everybody calls me Zizi. Can I help it?" He turned to a shelf behind his bar and produced an envelope. "Here is your message/' he told Ross. "No one came to ask after you. You are not, perhaps, as popular as you think."

The inspector barked. "Enough! Just listen to me, my friend, and answer my questions truthfully. This is a serious business."

Zizi listened, but the questions produced nothing. He admitted that the man with the twisted neck may have been in the café on a previous occasion, but it was true, nevertheless, that he had never seen him before in the sense that he had not noticed him. Around noon, for example, the place was usually crowded. Many came and went. In a week a dozen men with twisted necks might demand service. What was absolutely certain was that he had never seen the girl before. Nor had he ever heard of anyone called Margolies. Slim, elegant foreigners with musician's fingers did not patronise the *Café des Lauriers*. The clientele was made up of honest folk, with or without twisted necks, but above all honest.

"If you think I have anything to do with your criminals, you are making a big mistake." Zizi banged the zinc with a clenched fist. "My nose is clean, now as always."

"Keep it that way," Guizet advised him. "And if your customer of last night appears again, you will do yourself a favour by informing me."

"We got what I expected," he confessed to Ross as they walked down the steep hill to the car. "The man is a rogue and a liar. The list of his accomplishments is long, but we have never been able to make a case against him. I will assign a man to go regularly to his wretched café. And now, Monsieur Barnes, if you will return with me to my office, we will see if there is any news about your vessel."

There was none. Not a word. The sea might have swallowed *Roselle* without a trace.

As Ross walked away from the Commissariat, a fresh anxiety came to reinforce the sick despair which had taken possession of him.

Except for the clothes he wore and the small stock of francs and traveller's cheques he had brought ashore with him, everything he possessed was in *Roselle*. He counted his money. Five thousand, four hundred and eighty-seven francs and ten pounds in cheques. In a few days he might well be stranded. Unless, of course, he could count on the balance of the charter money. That, according to the agreement, should be waiting for him at Lloyds Bank. So far all the monetary obligations had been fulfilled. Was it possible that . . .?

He began to hurry.

Yes, it was just possible that Margolies had completed the terms of the charter. Even if he had intended from the first to steal *Roselle* he might still have thought it prudent to secure himself against a checkup with the bank.

Yet, almost as soon as he had realised the possibility, Ross knew that he was doomed to disappointment. Margolies had been at pains to stipulate that *Roselle* should be brought into port between five and six in the evening. And that arrangement, faithfully carried out, had precluded an immediate visit to the bank. Margolies had secured himself all right.

The bank soon confirmed the fact. They had had no instructions from either Margolies or Flavius. The manager suggested that there had probably been some hitch or accidental omission. The branch had had dealings with Mr. Flavius in the past, and he had invariably been most scrupulous and reliable. Doubtless the matter would be rectified as soon as he arrived in Cannes that day.

Ross did not tell him that Mr. Flavius would not be arriving at Cannes that day. Everybody in the place would soon know all about it. And everybody in London, too. The disappearance of such an important international figure would be cabled round the world as soon as the first reporter heard about it. Eleanor and Tom Peters would read the news in the early editions of the evening papers.

He shivered under the hot sun.

They would read of the theft of *Roselle*, of the shooting of Tiny Kane. They would be in a panic about Ralph.

The least he could do was to send them a telegram. Yet what could he say? That everything was fine?

DISREGARD SENSATIONAL REPORTS STOP CONFIDENT RALPH IS SAFE STOP EXPECT HIS RETURN HOURLY STOP WILL WIRE NEWS INSTANTLY

It was not very truthful and anything but reassuring, but it would have to do. Of one thing they could be quite sure. He would move heaven and earth to save Ralph from any danger.

Heaven and earth? The phrase almost made him smile. He could not even move one inspector of police.

He went to the post office, wrote out the telegram and handed it in. Then he turned back to the Suquet again and climbed the hill to the *Café des Lauriers*.

Zizi eyed him coldly and banged about a little behind the bar, but made no verbal demonstrations of hostility.

Ross ordered a beer and sat near the door. He knew that what he was doing was futile. He might wait till doomsday, he would not see the man or the girl in this place again. Yet there was nothing else he could do.

When at last he moved, he went to the telephone and called Guizet. The inspector said there was still no news. He spoke impatiently as if a hundred other matters were engaging his attention.

"I will get in touch with you at your hotel immediately I hear anything."

"I can't stay in the hotel all day," Ross answered irritably. "If I am out, leave a message."

And he could not stay in the café all day. After an hour or so, he went on up the street to the top of Mont Chevalier and looked out over the sea from the ancient tower. A few yachts were sporting in the roadstead, and far out, passing the Lérins, a small naval craft, the size of a corvette, was steaming slowly on a south-easterly course.

Corsica? It was quite possible that the fugitives had made for Corsica, to seek hiding somewhere along its rugged coast. If so, and if all they had to worry about was that corvette, they were sitting pretty; safe for at least a week.

Or so it seemed to the tortured mind of the watcher.

A plane came speeding from the direction of Cap Roux, swung inland, and doubled back over the Estérel.

Sightseeing at a thousand francs a ride!

If he had the means, he could hire a plane. Then, he thought bitterly, he would be able to take a wider view of an empty sea.

He went down the hill again. He scanned the face of every passer-by in the forlorn hope that he might encounter the man or the girl who had been in the *Café des Lauriers*. He walked in the market place where the morning shopping crowds were now at their thickest. Twice he saw what he thought was the figure of the girl in the distance, but when he pressed forward the face was the wrong face.

Then, in the Rue Grande, he did see her. She came from a side street, turned in his direction, faltered, wheeled swiftly, and crossed the road in front of a car that had to swerve to avoid her.

She had recognised him. There was no doubt about it. Just as certainly she was anxious to avoid a further meeting with him.

He hurried across the road after her. He could overtake her at will, but there were a lot of people going and coming along the street and he wished to wait till he could approach her in a quieter spot. In the moment of recognition he had felt a leap of excitement, but now he was quite calm, knowing that she was in his hands.

She would cause him trouble, of course. She might contrive to make a scene, and if so it would be handy to have a policeman in sight. He could appeal for help and have her brought to Guizet. Or, if she sought help herself and made a charge against him, she would have to go along with him to the police poste. Either way would suit him.

He was ten yards behind her, ready to press forward at the right moment, when she turned the corner of a street that led towards the Boulevard Carnot. She entered a shop and he hurried to the entrance. It was a small shop that sold ribbons and laces and miscellaneous articles of feminine attire. He had the fear that there might be another doorway through which she might pass in the hope of evading him, but when he looked inside he was reassured. He had but to wait for her, and she must return to the street.

Her action, no doubt, had been thoughtless; a fling of desperation or panic, an impulse to gain time or to postpone the inevitable meeting. Yet she had an appearance of ease as she waited to be served. And now he had not the slightest doubt of her identity, for he was close to her and could see her very clearly through the doorway. She turned towards the street for an instant and he saw in her blue eyes the same troubled look with which she had come to his table in the *Café des Lauriers*.

Two counters ran the length of the shop, and at the rear was a glass-faced cash desk. The space between the counters was narrow and some of it was occupied by display tables of fancy goods and fabrics. Three assistants - a man and two women - were attending to customers. The girl and an elderly woman were waiting.

Ross strolled on a few yards and returned. The girl had moved farther along the counter, and again he had the fear that there might be some rear doorway through which she might escape.

He hesitated. This was no place in which to challenge her. If he tried it, he might play into her hands. She would be indignant. She would appeal to the manager or floor-walker or whatever the fellow was. She would demand protection from the attentions of the importunate stranger, and, in the resulting argument, might manage to elude him. Certainly he could not risk a repetition of the sort of interference he had suffered in the *Café des Lauriers*. Equally he could not risk the possibility that she knew of some other exit from the shop.

She was right at the back, near the cash-desk now, feeling the texture of some fabric that was draped from a stand on the last table.

Ross hesitated no longer. He had to be closer to her, to be sure of her. If she persisted in making a purchase, he, too, would make a purchase. A collar-stud, if they had such a thing. Or darning wool.

He entered the shop, and she darted across the floor towards the end of the counter. Then he saw the door in the side wall. He was running before she had it open, but he was too late to reach her. She was quick in movement, very quick. The door slammed behind her. He heard the cries of astonished women and the manager's voice raised in sharp protest.

"Monsieur! Monsieur!"

He sent a bolt of cloth flying as he dodged the manager and hurled himself at the door. He tugged at the handle before he realised that the barrier was held by a spring latch. He turned the small knob and pulled the door open.

Then he was in a narrow alley between two buildings. He ran to the right, towards the street from which he had come. She must have gone that way, and she could be no more than a few yards ahead of him. But when he reached the pavement there was no sign of her, and she had had no time to hide, no time to reach the entrance of another shop.

Desperately he wheeled and ran back along the alley. He had chosen the wrong direction, but, now, surely he had her trapped in the dead-end at the back of the shop.

The astonished manager, still protesting, was in his path, but stepped back nimbly into the doorway when the careering lunatic shouted at him violently in a foreign tongue.

"Out of the way!"

Ross ran on. A few paces beyond the door the alley opened into a yard full of empty packing-cases and cartons, but it was no dead-end. A gateway gave on to a lane that was almost blocked by an unattended delivery truck. He squeezed past the vehicle, pursued by the manager.

He saw a wide street at the end of the lane. He went on with all the speed that he could get out of his pounding feet, confident that he would soon overhaul his quarry. When he reached the street, she was twenty yards away from him, but all he saw of her was the last swing of her skirt and a glint of nylon as she stepped into a taxi.

"Wait!" he yelled at the driver. "Wait!"

With a disdainful backward gesture of one hand the man rejected the demand. Wasn't it plain to see that he was engaged?

The cab trundled with slowly gathering speed towards the Boulevard Carnot.

Ross ran after it, hoping to find another cab and give chase, but the hope was a forlorn one. Cruising hackneys were rare in Cannes, and it was just by sheer chance that the girl had been able to intercept one on its way back to the stand in front of the railway station.

Still Ross ran on, and only halted when he reached the wide space before the road-bridge over the railway. There was no vehicle for hire nearer than the station, and, although this was in sight, it was too far away for his purpose. The taxi with the vanishing lady inside bowled along over the bridge and up the boulevard towards Le Cannet, and all Ross had for dubious consolation was a mental note of the number on the rear plate.

When he looked back, the shop-manager, a diminutive figure in the distance, shook an angry fist at him.

Chapter 11

Inspector Guizet was not very encouraging. He looked harassed, and definitely he was slightly out of temper. Possibly he saw already, or it may have been pointed out to him from a higher level, that the Flavius case had aspects to cause him insomnia, and the thought that Monsieur Barnes might cultivate the habit of popping in at any odd moment was not a welcome one. He listened a little impatiently, but acted promptly when he had heard the whole story.

"The driver will be questioned as soon as he returns to his rank or his garage," the inspector announced. "The result will come in with the least possible delay, but, if this is really the woman you saw in the café, I doubt if she will be driven to the place where she lives."

"Why should she have acted as she did if she were not the woman?" Ross demanded.

"She saw that you were following her. She may have wished to avoid unwelcome attentions. Some women are very nervous in certain circumstances. If you wish to, you may wait, but I am very busy."

Ross waited. The report came in with astonishing rapidity, and Guizet was then the first to admit that the fleeing fare had behaved suspiciously.

Her first instruction to the cabby was to take her to Le Cannet and to make all possible speed. She was late for an appointment, she had said, but, when half the distance had been covered, she ordered her man to take the road to the right across the viaduct and return by the Boulevard d'Italie. She said she had forgotten something and must go home, but gave no address. At the corner of the Rue de Châteaudun she stopped him and paid him off. That was all he knew.

"Châteaudun?" Guizet meditated aloud. "It is certain then that she does not live in that section, if she lives in Cannes at all."

Ross took his own meditations into the sunlight, turning his back on the Commissariat. If she lived in Cannes, she would be moving out. It was too small a town. She would not expose herself to the risk of another chance encounter.

Quite oblivious of direction, Ross wandered aimlessly till he found himself in the Rue d'Antibes. Then he was reminded that he had to buy some things to wear. He told himself that he must shop cautiously, to save his francs, and he tried hard to keep his mind on the task.

When he had his parcels, he started towards his hotel, but somewhere along the way he must have wheeled about, for, instead of the hotel, he arrived at the corner of the Rue de Châteaudun where the girl had paid off her taxi.

What he could hope for from this visit, he did not know, unless he imagined that something might put him on her trail. Which was absurd, and the longer he stood there the more absurd it seemed.

There were so many ways she might have taken. Across the market place and down towards the sea. Or along to the station to board a train for somewhere, anywhere. Marseilles, perhaps. Or Ventmille and so into Italy.

Speculation was profitless. Ross moved from the corner, crossed the railway, and walked with a purpose up the Boulevard d'Italie. The people on the pavement increased a sense of solitariness that had suddenly become an affliction, yet the way was familiar to him. When he was last here, he had had a friend.

The wine shop on the corner beyond the Mimont was still there. So was the lean, lugubrious dispenser who looked like that character of the posters who was always confronted by acute problems in terms of bottles. There was no glint of recognition in the gloomy eyes that gazed across the counter.

"I am looking for my friend Varenine," Ross said.

The grunt in reply might have been unintelligible if it had not been expected.

"Max le Russe?"

"Exactly. You remember me?"

The question passed unnoticed. "He comes here no more."

Ross was full of disappointment. "He has left Cannes?"

"He has gone from the Prado. You will find him, no doubt, at the Casino each night, with his latest system."

Relief in Ross was large. Russian Max had become peculiarly important to him.

"Then he goes on with his work?"

"Work?" The word brought increased melancholy to the shopkeeper. "He no longer goes to the harbour to repair the engines. He drops his tools as he drops his old friends. He flies high, that fellow. They say he has bought an aeroplane. It may be true. He no longer buys his wine from me. He is too big for that. He has become a great entrepreneur, a millionaire. Soon he will own all the Midi. You will be fortunate if he remembers you. Or unfortunate."

"But . . ."

"Yes, yes, yes. He has come into money. One day his system worked. Next day he went to Monte Carlo, and still it worked. He came to pay me what he owed - fifty-seven litres of vin rouge. Then he took his thirst elsewhere. I, you see, was merely an old friend. I gave him drink when he was dying of a parched gullet. I fed him when he was starving. What do you desire?"

"A glass of red."

He was as thirsty as ever Max had been. He drank and walked out into the sun. Gloom followed brief encouragement. The old man's report of Max had been too destructive.

The hotel was an unfriendly place, a cheap lodging for itinerants who came in by late trains or had early ones to catch. Ross went to his room, dropped his parcels on the bureau, and stretched himself on the bed.

Weariness of mind combined with fatigue of body to produce a state of exhaustion. He needed sleep, but for a long time he merely dozed between spells of complete wakefulness in which he listened to every step in the corridor. He might be called to the telephone at any moment to hear news from Guizet, but always the steps passed on. At last he fell into a deep sleep, and it was late when he came out of it. Knuckles were rapping loudly on a door. Not his door.

He phoned the police, but Guizet was not in. An assistant informed him that a plane was bringing a group of investigators from the Sûreté Nationale in Paris, headed by one of the most distinguished officers. A celebrity, in fact. But the disappearance of Monsieur Flavius was a sensation of the first magnitude. Already there were international repercussions. The Paris Bourse had had a hectic day. The Stock Exchange in London was a place of raised eyebrows, Wall Street had closed in a ferment.

"When will the inspector return?" Ross demanded when he could get in a word.

The assistant did not know. It was certain that Monsieur Guizet would be occupied with Chief-Inspector Laurent of the Sûreté till a late hour. The plane was expected at six. Monsieur Barnes must have faith. The great Laurent would soon be on the job.

It was nearly six. At ten minutes past the hour a telegram arrived from London.

WIRE IF ANY NEWS STOP EXPECT LEAVE FOR CANNES TOMORROW - ELEANOR

He might have foreseen it. He realised only too clearly how distressed she must be about Ralph, but she could do nothing by bringing her sick anxiety to this place. She would be an additional worry, an impediment. He would have to look after her, and that, in her state of mind, would be a full-time job.

An urgent reply was necessary. He walked to the post office and wired her that investigations were progressing and that she must not come to Cannes.

He stopped at a small café. He had to get some food inside him or he could not keep going, but he had no appetite. After a simple meal he returned to the hotel, hoping that Guizet might call him and give him some news. He waited. But Guizet, of course, would be tied up with the head serang from the Sûreté, and meanwhile, it seemed, that everything must be at a standstill.

What the devil was the French Navy doing that it couldn't pick up a mark like *Roselle* in all the hours that had passed?

Margolies must have bolted for Corsica. Margolies had had it all planned from that very first day of his visit to the yard. He had measured up *Roselle* with the one purpose in mind. Margolies knew the Diesels and what they could do. Margolies's fine long fingers might have suggested a musician, but they could play tunes with engine-oil and cotton-waste. And those same fingers had moved delicately over a chart, plotting a voyage within the range of a night's run.

Calvi, for instance. But not the port. Somewhere, some hidden cove or rocky inlet between Calvi and Ajaccio.

Ross went downstairs again and spoke to the clerk at the desk. "If Inspector Guizet telephones, please inform him that I have gone to the Casino. I expect to return early. Should he wish to reach me before, he will know where to find me."

It was not yet eight when he arrived at the Casino. In the entrance he halted an attendant he knew by sight.

"Does Monsieur Varenine still come here?"

The answer was given without hesitation. Everybody in the establishment knew Russian Max. Certain it was that he still came here, but not so frequently. Nowadays he was a busy man. But very busy. Perhaps, if monsieur had time to wait . . .

Monsieur could make time. He loitered near the entrance. It was an off night. Tomorrow there would be a grand concert with a great violinist and no less than three distinguished stars of the opera. Tonight the theatre was closed.

Ross read the announcement. The name of the violinist was faintly familiar. He had never heard of the distinguished opera stars, Gina Ferrani, Alicia Mars, Raoul Muys. Possibly nobody had ever heard of them outside a circuit of small provincial theatres. They came up from Italy or down from the schools of Paris in and out of season. Some of them might be good.

But what, in the name of heaven, did it matter to him, except that for a moment they broke in on his gloom with their gay-sounding names? Gina Ferrani, Alicia Mars. They were young and possibly lovely and full of hope. They had not sent a favourite nephew into danger or lost a craft into which they had put their last pennies. Across the foyer they stared out of a glazed showcase with their stage smiles turned on, but he did not go closer to investigate.

People were coming in from the Croisette; others were emerging from the restaurant. Somewhere an orchestra played a cooing waltz scored for strings. Ross scanned faces eagerly.

He waited. He shifted his position. The lobby filled and cleared, filled and cleared. He moved again, and at last he was rewarded. Max Varenine came loping towards him from the street.

"Ross! My dear Ross! Ever since I read the news I have been racing all over Cannes trying to find you!"

Max embraced him in an emotional Russian way, so he took it that he was not among the forgotten friends.

"I came here to look for you," Ross said. "I saw old Boileau in his shop. He told me about your good fortune."

"I imagine. I know what the wily scoundrel has been saying. It is poppycock. I won a little money. I invested it. Now I work harder than ever in my life to keep from bankruptcy. But there is time for my affairs. I must know about your catastrophe. I must help you if I can."

He looked for a quiet place and found it in the foyer, close to the smiling faces of the distinguished opera stars in the show-case.

Ross told his story. Max was sympathetic. He had not changed, except that the peculiarly permanent furrows of his brow seemed to have deepened. He was a little leaner, a little greyer, but as overwhelmingly vital as he had always been, with the same clamouring impatience that made him cut in with the next question before you could fully answer the last, with the same inclination of his head as if he must stoop from his abnormal height to catch what you were saying.

Abnormal? He was more than a head above Ross and as lean as a barber's pole, and his suit was cut on spare lines as if some anxiety to accentuate the lack of girth had entered into the planning of it. There were times when he looked like a clean-shaven Quixote in modern dress, but there was nothing woeful about his countenance. The mouth had a gay lift, and the eyes under the tufty brows were rarely without a pale blue glint of humour. Now they were all anxiety for his friend.

"First I must get you out of that hotel," he decided. "To-morrow you will come to me as my guest. I have a flat, now, with a spare bed. I could not endure that room on the Prado any longer. The bell of the church was ever ringing in my ears. The nightingales kept me awake all night. I know now what Gogol meant when he spoke of their clamour. The Ukraine is a place to avoid; so too is the neighbourhood of the Pezou when those infernal birds hold their concert."

Ross was no longer listening. He stared at a photograph in the glazed showcase of the concert artists. He moved towards it as if he had forgotten Max Varenine. He glanced at the name under the picture, then focused on the face as if it were something unbelievable.

"Pardon," Max said. "I babble. The lady is Alicia Mars. Why are you so interested? It is not possible that you know her. She came up from the San Carlo last year for the opera season. Her voice is not so good, but she is very beautiful and acts charmingly. She made a very nice Musetta. You see that she is wearing the costume."

"Mars is not an Italian name."

Max shrugged. "I know an Italian named Higgins. If you wish, I will get seats for the concert to-morrow night. She will sing Musetta's Song and the Gavotte from '*Mignon*.' "

"Tomorrow - "

Ross felt a hand on his shoulder and swung round.

Inspector Guizet said: "I learned from the hotel that you were here. I am in a hurry, so I have come to fetch you."

"You come at the right moment!" Ross exclaimed excitedly, and he pulled Guizet forward and pointed. "That is the woman of the *Café des Lauriers*."

"Monsieur Barnes!" The inspector sounded a shade impatient. "It is understandable in the circumstances, I admit. You are worried, you carry a great burden of anxiety, but I pray that you will not see this woman in every face you encounter. This morning it was somebody in the street. Now - "

"It is the same woman," Ross broke in. "You have only to find her and bring her in."

"There is something more urgent." Guizet was stubborn in disbelief. "Chief-Inspector Laurent of the Sûreté is waiting in the car. We are on the way to the *Hotel Marinville* and we wish you to come with us. Monsieur Caton Margolies has returned from Marseilles just as he promised in his telegram to Juan-les-Pins."

"Returned?" Ross put all his amazement into the questioning echo. "How can it be possible if he . . ."

"That is what we wish to discover." There was a new dryness in Guizet's voice. "He was on the telephone to headquarters the moment he arrived. He started from Marseilles before the papers came out with the news. He says he heard nothing till he reached Cannes."

Ross turned to Max Varenine in his bewilderment.

"You had better go at once," Max advised him. "I will call for you at your hotel in the morning."

Guizet introduced Ross to Chief-Inspector Laurent. The man from the Sûreté responded with a stare and an unamiable grunt. He had a heavy, sagging face under a wide-brimmed black homburg. Ross felt, rather than saw his bulk in the shadowy back of the car. A large man, round, with no neck; only a thin white collar to show where the torso left off and the head began. When they drew up at the *Marinville*, Laurent heaved himself out with another grunt and started up the steps as if he wished to dissociate himself from his companions.

The Flavius party had transferred from Juan-les-Pins. They were all there, in the suite reserved for their missing employer - Miss Blieke, the stenographer; Schuper, the valet; Delbert, the chauffeur.

Miss Blieke was in a bad state of nerves. She looked at the bulky Laurent as if she saw in him something terrifying. She made a gesture with a trembling hand. Her eyelids fluttered. You would have thought she had been invited to put her head on the block.

"Mr. Margolies is waiting," she said. "I'll tell him."

A tall, well-built man came from an inner room. He had a young-looking face, but his hair was quite white. Another secretary, perhaps.

Ross, keyed-up to confront his charterer, felt a sudden let-down. This one had nothing that could be described as elegance. His fingers were podgy, his accent was strongly American. If he favoured any instrument, it must be a horn or a saxophone. And he wasted no moment on preliminary courtesies.

"It's about time you came," he shot at the group of visitors. "I want to know what you've done and what you're doing. I hope you realise that this is a calamity. I return here to find that my chief has been carried off by a gang of kidnappers. I am not here ten minutes when this" - he waved a sheet of paper before them - "this is pushed under that door there. This!"

Madeleine Blieke uttered a cry, pawed with her right hand, sank to her knees, and keeled over on the carpet in a dead faint.

"Do something, Schuper!" the white-haired man commanded sharply. "Get her to her room. Give him a hand, Delbert. Get water. Get brandy. Get a doctor."

"Yes, Mr. Margolies." The valet jumped to it. "At once, Mr. Margolies."

Ross jumped, too, but not to give first aid.

"But," he cried, "you are not Margolies!"

"Not Margolies!" The surprised exclamation was accompanied by a movement of the arms that signalled a final despair. "Of course I'm Margolies! Who the devil do you think I am?"

Chapter 12

No one showed any emotion except Ross. Chief-Inspector Laurent swivelled his head slightly on his torso and made a small guttural noise. Guizet nodded. "I suspected it," he said.

"What did you suspect?" the white-haired man demanded. "That you were not the other Margolies."

"I don't know what you are talking about."

The real Margolies seemed to be holding himself in by an effort. "There is some nonsense about my having chartered a boat. Perhaps I have not had time to grasp everything."

Guizet began to explain, but he was too deliberate and longwinded for Margolies, who interrupted him.

"All right," he snapped. "So one of the gang impersonated me. That is enough for the moment. Here is something more urgent."

He flourished the disturbing sheet of paper again. "It is in English. I had better read it to you." He read it, he translated it, he handed it over.

The message was made up of words and sometimes individual letters cut from a newspaper and pasted on the sheet. It said:

Flavius is safe. To keep him so, follow instructions. Get ready a hundred thousand Swiss francs in hundred-franc notes and wait.

Guizet frowned. "It is curious they do not tell you to keep quiet about it. You are wise, in any case, to let us know."

"I want your advice, naturally. The next note may order me to act alone." Margolies turned to Ross. "You, I take it, are the officer from Paris?"

Guizet corrected the misapprehension and made introductions. Margolies gazed dubiously at Ross, then switched to the bulky celebrity of the Sûreté.

"What do you think, monsieur?" he demanded.

Laurent spoke for the first time.

"I think a hundred thousand Swiss francs is very cheap for a millionaire."

"So we're dealing with a set of cheap crooks."

The great man returned to the inarticulate, as though the effort of speech was too difficult to pursue. His grunt had a decidedly negative sound. He raised a heavy hand and tugged at the thin collar under his chin. He wore a narrow white tie in the style of the late Monsieur Laval, but there was no other resemblance.

Emerged from the shadowy interior of the police car and the shelter of his black homburg, he was a glum and serious citizen. Having heard nothing of his prowess, you might have put him down as a prosperous wine-merchant struggling with the problems of a provincial mairie. Not much hair was left to him. Most of it consisted of a suspiciously lustrous lick that straggled across a shining pate. The face was suety. Small eyes peered from creases in the puff pastry that hid the bone structure, and under a button of a nose the full lips of a narrow mouth seemed eternally pursed between the encroaching folds of the cheeks.

Guizet addressed Margolies. "Do you intend to meet this demand for ransom?"

"I would like the opinion of Monsieur Laurent."

The man from Paris spoke again. His voice was a reedy treble. "Why did that woman faint?" he asked.

"Mademoiselle Blieke? She's highly strung. She's had a nerve-racking day on top of the shock. What do you expect?"

"I expect nothing. I merely observe. You wave a paper, and she drops to the floor. Had she seen the message?"

"No. It was in an envelope addressed to me, marked confidential."

"Yet you produce it in front of her, and in front of the two men, Schuper and Delbert."

"The staff is entirely trustworthy. They would do anything for the chief."

"There has been too much trustfulness already. Monsieur Barnes, here, has been made the victim of his own trustfulness, if his deposition is true. Mr. Flavius walked out of his hotel so trustfully last night, and that seems to me a most peculiar thing."

"Why Is it peculiar?"

Monsieur Laurent waited, needing, perhaps, a reserve of supporting breath for another sally in loquacity.

"Clandestine is the word," he announced. "Trustfully clandestine. He dismisses the trustworthy staff and walks out alone, though customarily he is guarded by the chauffeur, Delbert, lately of the Foreign Legion and some time amateur champion in the light-heavyweight class. Wait!" He held up a ponderous hand as Margolies was about to break in. "That, in Monsieur Flavius, is peculiar, especially when it is remembered that he is on the eve of a financial deal involving many millions."

"What do you know about that?" Margolies did not like it.

Laurent's fat hand moved in a lateral sweep of dismissal. "Monsieur Margolies, I am the expert of the Sûreté in cases involving finance," he wheezed modestly. "I study finance. I weigh up all the rumours, printed and imprinted. I hear bird voices in the trees. I keep my ear glued to what you call the grapevine. Why did you suddenly dash off to Marseilles last night?"

"That has nothing to do with the matter."

"No? You went to see Sophocles, leaving your chief to deal with Aristotle. Who are these Greeks?"

"You need not concern yourself with a telegram in a private code."

"I have orders to concern myself with the disappearance of Monsieur Flavius. I have your telegram from Marseilles referring to your Operation Bouillabaisse. Moussaka would have been a more appropriate dish, perhaps. If I identify Monsieur Merle-Florac as Aristotle, I proceed to the conclusion that Sophocles is also an important financier."

"You had better concern yourself with the thugs who are holding Flavius."

"We will come to the thugs, I hope. Meanwhile, let us concentrate on Sophocles. A certain Mr. Smith made a hurried trip from London to Marseilles yesterday, using a private plane. I think you are aware of his true name. I am. I am also aware that he represents an association of English manufacturers who have an alliance with certain American interests."

"You are not suggesting that such people would be concerned in this outrage?"

"Certainly not. I am merely suggesting that Mr. Smith is the Sophocles of your telegram, and that the attack on Monsieur Flavius is by people of another sort, people who are anxious to put through an international scheme of their own by grabbing the foundations before the ground floor is laid."

"People who demand a ransom of a hundred thousand francs?" Margolies inquired dryly. "If they were after big deals in shares, they wouldn't bother about such chicken feed."

"It's the chicken feed that makes me suspicious." Chief-Inspector Laurent blinked his small eyes. "The only point that troubles me is the bad psychology."

"Perhaps you should trouble less about psychology. This is just a gang of small-time bandits after a bit of quick money. Nowadays the Riviera keeps its jewels locked up, so they turn to a spot of kidnapping."

"And for this they send a man to London to charter a suitable craft, bring it down by sea, arrange fuelling credits, set an elaborate time-table, murder a man . . .?" Laurent ran short of breath. "No, no, no," he gasped. "You must not delude yourself, Monsieur Margolies. For that matter, I wonder if you do. When you have had time to think things over, we will have a little talk about this Operation Bouillabaisse and the other affairs of Monsieur Flavius."

"There's nothing more I can tell you." Margolies was nettled. "There may be a clue in the ransom note. Why don't you get busy on that?"

Laurent held the sheet to the light. "A commonly used Montpellier bank; letters and words cut from the Herald Tribune and the Paris Daily Mail, Same device on the envelope, I suppose."

"Yes. I'll get it for you."

"There's no need." Again Monsieur Laurent made that lateral motion with his right hand. "You will let me know, perhaps, when you receive further instructions. For the moment I have much to do." He turned to Ross, swivelling his head slowly. "I would like, Monsieur Barnes, to see you in Inspector Guizet's office at ten in the morning. Is it convenient?"

"I shall be there," Ross answered promptly.

Laurent got up to go, and Guizet, a little bewildered, motioned to Ross to follow. At the door the financial expert of the Sûreté wheeled with the lethal abruptness of a Parthian in retreat.

"Your Mademoiselle Blieke, Monsieur Margolies," he said. "Is she subject to these fainting fits?"

The confidential secretary glared. He did not like Monsieur Laurent.

"Mademoiselle Blieke is a perfectly healthy girl," he retorted. "Under normal conditions she can meet all the requirements of her job."

"Then she will soon recover from her little indisposition." Monsieur Laurent looked into the depths of his black homburg with the slightly concerned air of a conjurer who has mislaid a rabbit. "Please let me know when she is quite well. Possibly after a night's rest . . ." He brought the sentence to a half close with one of his minor grunts. "I am obliged to you, monsieur. Quite obliged."

Chapter 13

Whether her night was restful or not, Madeleine Blieke must have been up fairly early in the morning, for she was with Chief-Inspector Laurent when Ross arrived at Guizet's office. And it seemed that Miss Blieke had had a long session with Laurent. At least she appeared to have had a mental mauling. She turned to Ross with a look that he interpreted as one of desperate appeal. Perhaps she had expected someone else. She half rose from her chair then slumped back, trembling. She had been crying. The signs of it showed in her eyes and also in the state of her make-up. A recklessly used handkerchief had drawn a smudge of lipstick in a downward curve from a corner of her mouth and she still held the handkerchief in a tight grip.

"That will be all, mademoiselle," Laurent told her in his cold, impersonal treble. "I want you to wait in the next room. When I have had a talk with Monsieur Barnes, I will see you again. Meanwhile, you will please think over my suggestion."

"I must go back to the hotel." The girl was on her feet, insisting desperately. "Monsieur Margolies will be waiting for me. The work is important."

"At the moment, my work is more important. The sergeant has instructions to see that everything is done for your comfort. If you would like coffee and something to eat, he will send out for it."

"I wish to use the telephone, at once."

"Not at once, mademoiselle. As soon as you have completed your statement, the telephone will be at your service, if you still wish to use it."

"I've nothing more to tell you. I've told you a hundred times that I've nothing more to tell you."

"Six times, mademoiselle. Six times. We must be accurate. You have not told me why you went to the bar in the Rue Flaubert and what you did there."

She was suddenly hysterical, hammering on the desk with tightly clenched hands. "I have told you. I wanted a drink."

"Yes. I have a note of it. You ordered a cassis. While you wait in the next room, we will ask the waiter if he remembers it."

"I demand that you let me talk to Monsieur Margolies."

"I will see if he is in. I will try to get through to the hotel as soon as a line is clear. But you know yourself that Monsieur Margolies wishes you to help us in every possible way. I am sure he will say that you may stay here till your statement is completed."

"You can't hold me here against my will. You'll account for it. Monsieur Flavius will see that you do. I won't tolerate this outrage."

"The outrage, mademoiselle, was when Monsieur Flavius was kidnapped. You're free to go if you wish to. I merely suggest that you wait. We have treated you with every consideration, and I can't see why you should be so concerned about such a small thing as a cassis. If I warn you against an action that may be regrettable, it is only in your own interest. Now be a good girl and get control of yourself."

Guizet shepherded her from the room. Laurent sifted some papers on his desk. "One moment, please, Monsieur Barnes. I must run through your first statement."

He started to run through it. Guizet returned. "She has decided to wait," he announced.

"Naturally." Laurent had been quite certain of it. "Lebas will be back from Juan-les-Pins with the waiter before I have done with our friend here." The bald dome with its straggling but lustrous lock made a suspicion of an inclination towards Ross. "The woman is lying. She was up to some mischief in that café. It is useless to frown at me Inspector. I know how to get the truth from such witnesses. I am overstepping no bounds. It is conscience that applies the torture."

Ross approved. He felt that he would get somewhere now that the quiet, hesitant Guizet had been pushed into the background. Laurent was shrewd. He could see a point at once. He would be ruthless in following a clue. Possibly he was over-suspicious about a natural agitation in Miss Blieke, but he was right to resolve any and every suspicion.

One mention of Alicia Mars, and he would demand tickets for to-night's concert. Ross would suggest that they go together.

Yet the thought of the consideration that Alicia Mars would receive from this man from Paris was somehow painful. Miss Blieke had been reduced to a deplorable state of collapse.

"Thank you, Guizet," Laurent said. "Will you please see that I am not interrupted?"

Guizet stared. To be turned out of his own office like this! He was about to protest. Instead, he walked out without a word.

Laurent grunted over the paper before him, pushed it aside, and focused on Ross.

"Why are you so certain that the boy Ralph is safe?" he demanded.

Assuredly he could see a point at once. Ross himself was slower in perception.

"Safe?" He raised his voice in pained surprise. "How could I be certain ? It's because of the boy that I'm so anxious."

"But you say he's safe?"

"No, sir. I wish to heaven I could say it."

"We have it in your own words, Monsieur Barnes." The assertion came clanging at him like a formal accusation.

"That is impossible," he retorted sharply.

Laurent leaned towards him, pressing against the desk. "The excellent Guizet has recovered a telegram which you sent to the boy's mother in London. It is here written in your own hand. 'Disregard sensational stories,' etcetera, etcetera. 'Confident Ralph is safe. Stop. Expect his return hourly.' "

"Naturally." Ross relaxed. "What else could I have sent? I knew everything would be in the London papers. I didn't want my sister to go off her head."

"Then it is a lie?"

"No. It is not a lie. Surely it's obvious . . ."

Laurent interrupted him shrilly. "If it is not a lie, it is the truth. You believe that the boy is safe. You assure the mother that he will soon be returned to you."

"But can't you see I merely wished to ease the shock for her?"

"I see your own words, monsieur."

Laurent was obtuse, or he was deliberately rejecting the explanation because of some bug that had bitten him. He hammered and hammered at the point, and Ross began to appreciate what must have happened to Madeleine Blieke. Also, he began to amend his view of Chief-Inspector Laurent, and, before the interrogation was over, had grown to dislike the man.

He lost count of the times Laurent took him over the business of that innocent telegram. It might have been six. It seemed like a hundred. At last Laurent switched to another point, and Ross suddenly realised, with cold alarm fighting hot indignation in him, that there was some logic if no reason in the procedure.

"Very well, Monsieur Barnes." Laurent grunted and pushed the telegram aside. "Let us come to the moment when you left the *Café des Lauriers* after your fantastic encounter with the woman stranger and her male companion."

Laurent scanned the deposition again, moving a stubby forefinger along the lines of typewriting. Here, in this pause, was the opportunity for Ross to assert that the woman stranger was Alicia Mars, but he did not respond to the cue. It could be because she was so like his lost Mary. It might be because the thought was developing that he must tackle Alicia Mars without the intervention of the police, for he was certain now that she would freeze before this ponderous monster from the Sûreté.

"Yes, yes, yes," the monster murmured. "It is all very clear in your own words. You left the café in an attempt to overtake the woman. You went back to the café to leave a note for the supposed Margolies, the American with the pianist's fingers. Then, surprisingly, you adjourned to a restaurant on the Rue d'Antibes and ate a leisurely meal."

"What's surprising about it? I had had nothing to eat and I was hungry."

"Hungry?" Laurent closed his eyes, thinking it over. "Monsieur Barnes, what I cannot understand is why, in the circumstances, you did not go back to your craft with the utmost speed. A woman you have never seen before calls you by your name and makes what you interpret as an appeal to you. Yet you behave as if no suspicion had entered your head. You smoke a cigar, you sip your Armagnac, and then, having allowed sufficient time for the pirates to seize your craft twice over, you stroll along to the wharf to discover that she is not there. All this because you say you were angry with the man who had chartered your craft on handsome terms!"

Ross was much more angry with Monsieur Laurent. "Are you trying to imply that I knew the craft was going to be used by the kidnappers?"

"I am trying merely to find the explanation of your strangely ready acceptance of a situation that was, at the very least, curious."

"Try the very simple explanation," Ross retorted. "I was kept kicking about and being kicked. I needed a meal. I reasoned that if the supposed Margolies wanted me, he could go to the jetty. If he had to wait a while, it was his own fault."

The simple explanation was not acceptable to Laurent. Ross saw that his behaviour had indeed been questionable, but he was not prepared to admit this. It was, of course, easy to see where one had erred after the event, only this was no plea to advance. Laurent would hold to his point, disregarding the fact that some human perverseness or aberration that seemed small at the time might easily be magnified out of proportion to the truth. Only the experts of the Sûreté were infallible.

He put the thought into words, but Monsieur Laurent made a modest gesture of deprecation. Monsieur Laurent believed that he had his victim at a disadvantage, and his persistence had a queer feline ruthlessness. He went back to the beginning, and behind every question he asked was the assumption that Ross had been the willing accomplice of the false Margolies from the moment of their first meeting. It was expressed not by the words he used, but by inflection, by innuendo, by phrasing that aimed at an unwary admission.

The cross-examination went on for an hour or more, punctuated by injunctions to Ross to answer calmly, to consider well before he replied, to bear in mind that the purpose of it all was to help Ross himself. And in the end, of course, Laurent returned to the telegram.

"If you have reason to believe, Monsieur Barnes, that the boy Ralph is safe, I suggest that you confide in me fully."

One more word and Ross would explode. The tension brought him a creeping sensation under his scalp.

He said: "I'd like to suggest that you start an organised search for my craft. That way you might save my nephew and Flavius and get hold of the man who shot Kane."

Laurent had the pained look of a chef whose dish has been condemned before the final basting.

"Very well." He wheeled back a groaning swivel chair and heaved himself up from the desk. "I will, for the time being, accept the argument that you were completely duped by this impersonator of Margolies."

"I've told you again and again that everything added up." The fuse was sparking now. "I made all the inquiries I could, and everything added up."

"And now the bill has to be paid." Laurent shrugged. "There we will leave it for the moment, monsieur. If you find the waiter at your elbow, you should not blame me." He touched a bell on the desk. "You will not, on any account, leave Cannes. If you change your hotel, you will be good enough to inform Inspector Guizet."

"Perhaps you would like to put me in a cell?"

The explosion had no more effect than a squib. Laurent turned to the uniformed sergeant as the door opened.

"I will talk to Mademoiselle Blieke again. Bring her back here," he ordered. Then to Ross : "Thank you, monsieur. I will give careful consideration to everything you have said. Everything."

Chapter 14

Max Varenine was waiting at the hotel. So were six or seven newspapermen, French, English and American. Max was getting on very well with them. Max seemed to get on very well with everybody. "I have been telling them that we are old friends," he informed Ross. "I tried to send them away, but they will not go without a statement from you. I advise you to be amiable, especially with the local boys. It's good publicity."

"It's fine publicity." Ross was grim. "I'd better tell them that the kidnapping was my idea, that I organised the whole thing, that I have Flavius upstairs, packed away in a suitcase."

"What is this nonsense?"

"Do you think it's nonsense? The great panjandrum from Paris doesn't. He believes I'm in on the plot."

Max looked incredulous, but before he could comment one of the newspapermen broke up the hurried conference. Ross answered questions, most of which related to the deception practised by the supposed Margolies in England. It was all very easy and friendly, but he was glad when it was over; and glad, too, to leave the hotel for the flat of the solicitous Max.

He called up Guizet at once and gave him the address, in the Rue des États-Unis. "Now you know where to come if you want to arrest me," he added.

"Relax!" Max advised him. "Guizet is a man who docs his best. Perhaps this Laurent also has good intentions. It serves no purpose to make them peevish."

Ross tried to relax. The flat was comfortably and handsomely furnished. In another mood he might have admired it. Certainly it was in remarkable contrast to the room Max had rented in the Prado.

"I won a modest sum," Max explained. "The mistake I made was to go back to flying. You have heard, perhaps, that I bought a plane, a Morane Saulnier, a war-surplus bargain. I run pleasure flights for the visitors - over the Estérel and round the Lérins. It is a difficult business, but it gives me a living. There are times when I wished I had spent the money and stuck to marine engines, but now, for your sake, I am glad I did not."

"Why for my sake?" Ross was puzzled.

"We have a plane. This morning a man I employ is taking up the sightseers. This afternoon the joy-rides are cancelled. This afternoon you and I will fly in a search for your vessel."

"Max!" Ross could find nothing to add to the name. Excitement and gratitude lifted his spirits.

"Last night I took out the charts. I figured that the crooks must have planned to be in some hiding-place before daylight yesterday. It seems to me that Corsica would have been their logical objective."

"It was my own thought, Max."

"But we must not be too hopeful. Perhaps Corsica is too obvious, yet it gives us a starting-point. Perhaps there has already been an aerial search, only it is always possible to miss a needle when there is a lot of hay. You, at any rate, will know your craft if we spot her. Now I must attend to some business. If you will be ready by one, I will call for you here. Meanwhile, if you wish to look at the map, it is on my desk there."

Ross spent most of what was left of the morning following the indented plan of Corsica's coast, and by three in the afternoon the carefully drawn lines of the cartographer were being translated into a reality of bays and coves and inlets seen from the air.

They picked up the coast just below Calvi and turned southward to begin their circuit. The plane was speedy and readily responsive to its pilot. Max knew just what it could do, and, flying low, he followed the weaving course set by capes, promontories and headlands, the jagged edging of a fantasy of peaks and pinnacles and the impenetrable green tangle of the maquis. Whenever he sighted a small craft he came near to buzzing it to give Ross a close view, but always Ross shook his head. They turned inland when feasible creeks and streams beckoned. They found a motor vessel almost hidden in one such creek. It had familiar lines, but it was not *Roselle*. The davits were wrong.

South of Ajaccio they saw a French naval plane proceeding northward, and it, too, was flying low and weaving along the coast as though it were on the same mission. Up the east side they had a straighter run. Then, as they neared Bastia, Max swung out over the sea to take a look at the smaller islands, but there was no reward. When they had completed the flight, Ross knew by the measure of his disappointment how high his hope had been.

Back in the flat, Max urged him not to loose heart. "There are many other places where we must search" he said.

There were too many other places.

And meanwhile there was the concert at the Casino.

They went together. When he saw again the picture of Alicia Mars, Ross was not as confident as he had been. If Max had questioned him, he would have admitted a doubt, and, in the crowded auditorium, the doubt became large. After the street episode of the previous day, it was inconceivable that the girl would present herself before the public, yet there was no printed slip in the programme to indicate that Alicia Mars had backed out of her engagement.

Misgiving continued to grow in him. He was in an agony of suspense as the other woman singer came on to the stage to open the programme with an aria from *Samson and Delilah*. He was certain of one thing. If Alicia Mars was in fact the girl of the café, he would know her the moment he saw her.

The *Habañera* from *Carmen* was added to the *Saint-Saens* aria. Then the violinist enraptured the audience with an interminable group of numbers. An encore was demanded. He had to come back to bow again and again, but at last he was allowed to retire, and now it was the turn of Alicia Mars.

Ross looked at his programme nervously. "*Me voici dans son boudoir* from *Mignon*." When he focused on the stage, a small man in a dress suit was stepping forward.

Not the accompanist.

The small man made an amateurish gesture with his right hand. "With deep regret I have to announce that Mademoiselle Mars is not able to sing for you to-night, because of a sudden indisposition.

He went on to say that the other singers would each be heard in additional groups, but Ross did not listen. Max was already on his feet.

"You were right/' he said. "This is much too strange, to be a coincidence. Come with me. We will get to the bottom of it."

He knew the small announcer. He insisted on seeing him, and he and Ross were led to a small room back stage.

"Dino, what is the matter with Alicia Mars?" he demanded. "My friend Monsieur Barnes is a friend of hers. We expected to see her here to-night."

"So did we." The subject was irritating to Dino.

"This sudden indisposition, is it serious? My friend is very anxious."

"It is serious if she wishes to sing at this Casino in future." Dino leaped from indignation to anger. "Perhaps she has a splinter in her little finger. I do not know." He turned to Ross. "Forgive me. You must understand that we have been left to face a very difficult situation, and without a word of explanation. If you are a friend of hers, perhaps you can explain. When did you last see her?"

"Yesterday morning." Max supplied the answer when Ross hesitated.

"She was here yesterday morning for a rehearsal with the accompanist. She was well. She made no complaint. When I went to her dressing-room to-night, just before the concert, she was not there. I made inquiries. No one had seen her. 'Still,' I said to myself, ' she will arrive in plenty of time.' But she has not arrived. I called the police, but no accident has been reported. A woman with whom she stays is not on the phone. I have sent a messenger. He has not yet returned."

"We will make inquiries at once, Dino. What is the address?"

"Madame Roger Segal. . . You do not know the address?"

"Monsieur Barnes has just arrived. He saw Mademoiselle Mars

only briefly in the street. It was here that he expected to meet her."

"I am sorry," Dino said. "We have a rule about addresses."

"But in your position you have discretion," Max argued. "Surely, in the circumstances . . . Monsieur Barnes is an old friend since the days when she sang at the San Carlo. You can see how anxious he is."

The address was given.

"Perhaps it will be useless," Max remarked as he hailed a taxi outside the Casino. "But we may learn something."

The driver knew the Villa Cerrito on the Boulevard d'Alsace. It was a small house, approached by a few yards of tiled pathway between beds of low shrubs. Madame Segal was an American, but not of the more affluent type.

"We have come straight from the Casino," Max announced, and Madame Segal obligingly concluded that the visit was official.

"Oh, dear!" she exclaimed. "I have just sent your messenger away. This is very distressing. I don't know whatever can have happened to Alice. She left here in good time. I would have gone with her, but I had to wait home for my daughter. She's been visiting with her sister in Lausanne, and she would pick to-night for her return. I can't even run out to call the police. I'm terribly afraid there has been an accident. Alice has been in such a mood all day, as if she didn't know what she was doing. I do hope she hasn't been badly hurt."

"No accident has been reported," Ross told her.

"Then what on earth has happened to her? She was all right when she left here, except for her mood. She told me she was going to walk along the Croisette. Now that I think of it, she went on along the Alsace instead of crossing the railroad to go down to the front. That's rather odd, isn't it? Perhaps suddenly she didn't know who she was. I've heard of cases like that. She may be wandering round Cannes with her memory gone. She has been very worried about something the last few days, but she wouldn't tell me. Do, please, do something about it."

So far as Ross could see there was nothing to be done. He was too late by an hour or so, and the pity of it was that the address might have been obtained the previous night. But Guizet and Laurent had intervened, and later the aerial search had distracted him from the pursuit of the girl.

It was useless, Ross felt, to prolong this interview with the talkative Mrs. Segal, but Max would not be drawn away. Max was curious.

"You have known Mademoiselle Mars a long time?" he asked. "You are very close friends?"

"I have known her, yes." Mrs. Segal hesitated. "It's my daughter Peggy and Alice who are close friends. They were at the same music school back home. Cleveland, I mean. Cleveland, Ohio. Alice is a Columbus girl. Peggy could tell you more about her. I don't know ..."

"Please go on, madame," Max urged.

But Mrs. Segal had been halted by a thought. She was suddenly suspicious, not of Max and Ross, but of her daughter's friend.

"She really has been strange, the last few days – sort of morose and keeping to herself. Of course, it's none of my business, but I do think she might have confided in me if she has really run off with that man."

"What man?"

"I don't know. I never saw him. I know she was meeting someone, and then she got into this dark, worrying mood." The thought was hounding the woman. "Wait a minute!" she exclaimed. "I'll be right back."

She went urgently from the room and they heard her running up stairs. She returned rather slowly, frowning, with anger growing from a feeling of injury.

"Her valise is gone," she said. "And her make-up case. I suppose I ought to tell you, since you're from the Casino. She must have sneaked out with them while I was marketing and checked them somewhere. I can't make out why she had to slip you up over the concert. If she had to run away, at least she might have kept her engagement first."

"Perhaps she had a good reason." Ross astonished himself by speaking in her defence.

"What reason?" Mrs. Segal was sad about it now. "It's very puzzling. The girl is crazy about her music. She'd give anything for a chance to sing. She was much more serious than Peggy. After Cleveland, she went off to Rome to study, and then she had a season in Naples, but I guess you know about that. We met her again when she came up here last winter. That was when I took this shack. Peggy wanted a year or two abroad, and my younger daughter was at school in Lausanne, so you see . . .? Alice stayed on here for the summer and we invited her to live with us. I liked her round the house. She's a sweet girl, but I always did find her a little secretive."

"How, secretive?" Max was the prompter.

"Well, we never did know anything about her family, except that her mother was dead. She seemed cut off, quite alone, as if she had no folks back home at all. I never saw a letter from America all the time she was with us, but she used to send off money to somebody. She was always buying mandates at the post office. I don't know if Peggy can tell you any more about her. I don't think so, but she should be home any minute now. You can wait if you wish to."

There was nothing to wait for. Mrs. Segal went to the door with them, still chattering.

"I never thought that Alice would run off like this without a word. Maybe she won't be gone for long. She has left her wardrobe trunk and most of her clothes, anyway."

Ross was silent as he walked from the Villa Cerrito with Max. He believed now that the girl's flight would take her back to Italy, and perhaps she was already across the frontier at Ventmille,

Max said: "It might take a year to find her in Italy. She knows the country. She has friends. Perhaps Guizet and Laurent will listen to you now that it is too late. By the time the Italian police start moving, Flavius will be dead or ransomed."

"So there is no need to talk to the police."

Max turned his head to take a sharp look at his companion.

"Let's get a drink," he suggested.

Ross picked up an evening paper in the café. There was nothing new about the kidnapping. Cables indicated growing excitement and apprehension among financiers in half a dozen countries. The Flavius empire, deprived of its constitutional head, was getting frightened. Caton Margolies had made a reassuring statement, but the ticker tapes were eloquent of anxiety.

Otherwise the space given to the story was taken up by the press interview with Monsieur Barnes. The report was fair enough. It ended with the news that Monsieur Barnes was at present the guest of M. Maximilien Varenine, director of Varenine Air Tours.

"Good publicity," Max commented.

"Was it necessary?" Ross asked. "We'll have those newshounds on our doorstep every day."

"I should keep my big mouth closed. I was just talking while we waited for you."

"It doesn't matter, Max." Ross was in no position to make reproaches. All the way to the flat, he was sorry he had spoken.

The concierge had a message. Monsieur Barnes was requested to telephone to Inspector Guizet.

Ross felt heavy with tiredness, but he picked up the phone eagerly.

Guizet said: "If you are planning any more air trips with Monsieur Varenine, you had better consult me before you take off."

"So Laurent is having me shadowed?" Ross snapped back. "Is that it?"

"You are entirely wrong, monsieur, and you will permit me to say that you are a little over-sensitive. We have a routine man at the aerodrome. Incidentally, I can assure you that everything possible is being done to locate *Roselle*. We are quite confident that Corsica was not the objective of the kidnappers. The official surveys have been complete. They are continuing in other quarters, with special attention to the possibilities of concealment or camouflage."

"And there is no news?"

"Not from the air. We have talked to the waiter from the bar in Juan-les-Pins. lie says that Mademoiselle Blieke was with a dark woman when she had her cassis, but he is not able to describe her very well. He was busy at the time. Also, he is the next thing to a cretin. Mademoiselle Blieke says he is mistaken and insists that she was alone. It is strange, isn't it?"

"What is strange?"

"The distance between Juan-les-Pins and Cannes is not great. I think you told me that the woman in the *Café des Lauriers* had dark hair. By the way, I had a man check up on Alicia Mars. She was at a rehearsal yesterday morning. It lasted till well past the time when you saw the woman in the street." Inspector Guizet permitted himself a small chuckle. "You must be careful about your brunettes, Monsieur Barnes. There are too many of them at large."

Max poured drinks while he listened to an account of the conversation.

"You'd better get to bed, Ross," he advised. "You look all in. I'll wander along to the port to see what I can pick up. I might get a line on your friend with the twisted neck. Don't wait up for me. I'm likely to be late."

There was no change in the restless Max. Probably he would be gambling somewhere till the small hours. He swallowed his drink and went off.

Ross went to the bathroom to run a tub, but, before he could turn on the taps the phone brought him back to the living-room. The concierge spoke from his switchboard.

"Pardon, Monsieur Barnes, I forgot to tell you when you came in that a lady called early in the evening. She is here again. Shall I send her up to you?"

"A lady? But surely she wishes to see Monsieur Varenine?"

"No, no. She is asking for you. It seems she does not care to give me her name." The concierge lowered his voice. "She is English, I think. Her accent . . . One moment, monsieur."

Eleanor! In her anxiety for Ralph she must have taken a plane after all. He had telegraphed the name of his hotel. The desk clerk would have given her the new address.

The concierge spoke again. "The lady says it is urgent. She must see you at once."

"Send her up, please."

As he heard the drone of the lift with its whining overtone, he flinched at the thought of a painful meeting. He was on the landing when the cage stopped with a clang, and he saw through the metal lattice that the passenger was Alicia Mars.

Chapter 15

She was in a state of great agitation, afraid to face him now that it was too late for retreat. It seemed, indeed, that she thought of retreat, for she made a swift movement of one hand towards the buttons that worked the lift, but already he had thrown back the outer gate and was releasing the inner catch.

He saw her very clearly in the light from the top of the cage, observing every detail of her appearance in the first instant. A large-sleeved coat of a smooth, dark material hung loosely, cloak-like, from her shoulders, and when she reached towards the control panel it swung open, revealing a dark tailored suit with jacket buttoned over a white blouse. Under the light he saw the gleam of a black velvet cap and the glint of bronze in the lustrous waves of her dark hair.

Always, it seemed, there must be trouble in her face, but it added a touching appeal to her loveliness, and he was aware, with a tense, sudden awareness, that he could not resist that appeal. And now, under her fine brow, the large, wide-set eyes had a colouring of deeper blue. They were moist and tremulous, and she closed them for a moment as if she could not face him. A brief moment, and she opened them again. Then he saw the quivering of her half-parted lips. He waited, but she said nothing, and their eyes met.

It was a strange pause. She looked into his eyes, and he returned the gaze. He had been a little bewildered. After his vain search for her, she had come to him. There was some sort of special pleading in her eyes, and he felt his bewilderment change to elation. The pause lengthened. It seemed a long time, but perhaps it was not so long. Someone on another floor rang for the lift.

"Please," he said.

She moved from the cage and he closed the gates. He brought her into the flat and reached towards her to take her coat. She yielded it, perhaps without thinking, casually. It was so like a casual visit, but he saw that she was trembling. He was very close to her at that moment. He felt her isolation, and there was some sort of despair in it, a loneliness. Or an anxiety that made her desperate. She was immaculate in the dark slenderness of her beautifully fitted suit, yet he saw her pathetic in her distress and he had an impulse to comfort her.

"You are wondering why I am here," she said. "It must seem strange to you, after the way I avoided you yesterday."

"I was anxious to talk to you."

"Yes." She admitted the reasonableness of it. "Now I am putting myself in your hands. Two nights ago, in the *Café des Lauriers*, I tried to help you. It was not for your sake, but I'm hoping that you will remember it, because to-night I want you to help me."

She must have rehearsed the speech in her mind. Perhaps she had gone over the words many times, testing and changing them. Now they had a flat, artificial sound, but he did not question their sincerity.

"I've been trying to find you," he told her. "I went to the Casino to-night. Then to the Villa Cerrito."

She had expected it. "I knew it would be only a matter of time."

"Your friend Mrs. Segal is very disturbed."

"I'm sorry. I didn't know what to do. I've been nearly crazy. There seemed to be nothing to say till I had talked to you. I didn't know where to find you till I saw the newspaper to-night."

"Why didn't you go to the Casino for the concert?"

"I was in fear of what might happen. I had some wild idea of running away. I still have, but I'm in your hands. You can phone the police if you wish. They can't do much to me but make me talk. If you'll listen to me first, there might be some way out. I don't know."

They had been standing awkwardly near the doorway of the living-room. He made her sit down; he seated himself.

"If there's anything I can do . . ."

He pulled himself up because what he had started to say seemed absurd, a polite commonplace.

"I know," she said, reading his mind. "You think I'm mad to come to you. It's not for myself. It's for my brother. You saw him in the café with me. He's my half-brother, really. I tried to break up the thing that night. I thought if you were warned in time, you might interfere. I didn't know then how horrible it was going to be."

She hesitated. "I'm not going to soften things," she went on. "I want to explain. He was badly smashed up in the war. That changed him. He didn't go back home. He disappeared. I found him after a lot of trouble. In Milan. He was tied up with a group who were working some financial swindle. Petty. I got him out of it, but he wouldn't go straight. His new friends wouldn't let him."

Distress halted her. She had to make an effort to continue. "There was one man who seemed to have a hold over him, Alvaro Parra. He comes from the Argentine or Uruguay or somewhere, but he likes to be thought of as an American, a very polished American. You knew him in England as Margolies."

Ross had wondered about her purpose, had begun to question her story. She was an actress. She could turn on the tears. But suddenly he no longer had any doubt of her. There was a bitterness in her voice that could only be genuine.

"I don't wonder that he deceived you. He could impose on anybody. I thought myself that he was a trustworthy friend. He used to talk to me of music as if it were the one thing he cared about. He does care, but he uses that and everything else as stock in trade. He is a sharper, a confidence man, ready for any shady deal if the money is good enough. My brother used to tell me that he was harmless. I know now how dangerous he is."

"You mean that he organised the whole of this Flavius business?"

"I think in the first place he was hired. I don't know by whom. I don't know the purpose, except that there is some sort of business struggle against Flavius. I knew your vessel was going to be used. I found that out by accident. I tried to get my brother out of it, but he wouldn't listen. He said it was harmless. That was always his word.

They were going to take this American millionaire for a sea trip, and they were all going to make their fortunes. No one would be hurt. Flavius himself would not dare to take any action because his own crooked schemes would be exposed. It was the safest thing in the world."

She had been staring at the carpet. Now she met Ross's gaze.

"I didn't believe it," she cried. "But I couldn't go to the police and inform against my brother. When you saw me in the street yesterday, I wasn't aware of all that had happened. I didn't know a man had been murdered until I saw the afternoon papers. I had a great fear then that there would be more murder. And I knew that you must have given descriptions of us to the police. I found my brother in terror. I talked to him and argued and pleaded. In the end he agreed that we must help you to find your vessel. That way we thought you might be able to help us."

"How can I help you?" Ross rose from his seat and stood in front of her.

"You are the only one who could give evidence against us. But, if it became necessary, you could say we were not the two you saw in the *Café des Lauriers*."

He turned in agitation and walked to the window.

"The police are already satisfied that Alicia Mars was not the woman," he said.

"I'm not concerned for myself," she answered. "I want to save my brother. He will see you to-night. He will tell you all he knows. He will make a written statement and mail it to the police, or to yourself, if you wish. It will be unsigned, but it will be the truth. By the time it is delivered, he will be in Italy, if he is lucky. If he is held at Ventmille, you will say he is not the man."

It was her scheme, a woman's scheme. It was fantastic.

Ross looked out through the window, into the street, seeing nothing.

She sent her voice desperately across the room. "If you cannot agree, there is nothing more I can do. I have no knowledge myself. My brother will wait till eleven-thirty. After that he will try to reach Italy."

Her brother, her brother, her brother. Never a name to him.

"Where is your brother?" Ross asked.

"If you give me your word, I will tell you."

The ultimatum was clear. He turned to face her again.

"You seem sure that you can trust me."

"Yes."

In a final moment of silence, he heard the drone of the lift coming up again.

"Very well. I give you my word."

There was no sign of victory from her. She said: "Above the *Café des Lauriers* the street turns to the left. Higher up the hill there is a small alley, the Rue Tunis. The house is number nine and the room is on the top floor. You will find the name on the door. He calls himself Jean Seyrac."

The droning of the lift came to an end with a clang and a clatter outside the flat door. Then a key rattled in the latch, and Max Varenine came in.

He did not see the girl at once. He was too full of what he had to say.

"I've news, Ross. I hurried home to tell you. The port is full of it. Your *Roselle* has been picked up by a French naval vessel twelve miles north-east of Minorca. They're bringing her in to Cannes."

Ross had one thought. "Ralph?"

Max shook his head, staring past Ross at the girl. "Not a soul on board," he said. "They found her drifting, derelict. That's all. No details."

Ross was rigid, sinking, battling against the emptiness of dejection. The girl's voice broke in on the silence.

"You will go," she said. "It is more important now, and there isn't much time."

He answered her harshly. "You'll stay here till I get back." He turned to Max. "Look after her. You know who she is."

"Where are you going?"

"I can't explain. It's an appointment I must keep. It's a bargain. I shan't be long."

"But look here ..."

"You don't have to worry. It's all right."

"Yes." Alicia Mars supported him. "It's all right. I'll wait here for you."

There was reassurance in her voice and trustful encouragement in her eyes. He accepted her good faith. He had no mind any longer for judgment. Thoughts of Ralph and of the derelict *Roselle* shuttled about amid disordered fragments of her story, and he was governed only by the urgent desire to reach Jean Seyrac and learn what he could of the whereabouts of Ralph. To-morrow there would be action. Given the clue, the police would close in on Alvaro Parra and his accomplices. Laurent would see to that. Laurent, with his ruthlessness and drive, was the man for the job.

He had no great distance to go, but he looked for a taxi in the Rue d'Antibes. There was not a free cab in sight. He might find one in front of the station, but no time would be gained by making the detour. When he reached the Allées he ran, and in another minute he was hurrying up the steep ways of the Suquet. The Rue Tunis was a dark and dismal alley, a mere passage in the remoter burrows of the old town and the sight of the house brought him his first misgiving.

The girl's story might be false, designed to lead him into a trap, and there could be no better place for a trap. But he could see no motive for a trap. Alvaro Parra had brought off his coup and could have no further purpose to serve with him. The girl herself was a hostage in the hands of Max, and a willing hostage.

Ross struck a match to make sure of the number on the scarred plaster of the wall. He examined the doorway with another match, but it displayed no names of the tenants. The door opened when he turned the handle. A small bulb burned dimly in the narrow hall, disclosing at the rear a narrower staircase. No sign of a porter or janitor, but this was not a house for such frills. Possibly some sort of caretaker lived in the basement, and possibly you could summon him only by shouting. Anyway, Ross wanted no dealings with caretakers. His direction was clear. Jean Seyrac lived on the top floor.

The steps were of stone or concrete slabs. The banisters moved shakily to the touch. Ross climbed silently. Another dim bulb on the first landing showed him three doors. A murmur of voices and the cry of an infant reached him from behind one of them. The others were closed on silence.

A second flight led up into darkness. There were no more lights. The bulbs were dead or neglected. A smell of emptiness mingled with the odour of cooking oil and cabbage water and cheap tobacco.

Ross used matches. No switch was visible anywhere. When he reached the top floor he saw the name of Jean Seyrac on a card pinned to one of the doors. It was a clean card, reassuring. It had been placed there to guide him, since cards were not the mode in this dilapidation.

He rapped on the door. He rapped again. If the fellow had stayed here to wait for him, why didn't he answer? It was not yet eleven, and the time limit was eleven-thirty. Unless Alicia Mars had made a mistake . . .

A third time he rapped. Then he tried the handle.

The door opened.

He felt along the wall for a switch and found it. The room sprang up out of the darkness. A mean room with shabby furniture – a single bed with a painted iron frame, a grimy rep curtain of lime green slung unevenly from a triangular board to serve as a corner wardrobe, a chipped and battered chest of drawers, a broken-backed chair, bare boards, a neat suitcase.

Ross stared at the bed. There was something heaped on it under a stained pink counterpane; the form of a sleeping man, perhaps.

He called the name. "Are you there, Seyrac?"

Silence. There was no movement from the bed. The fellow was drunk or drugged, or . . .

Fear was in the air of the place. Ross moved back into the doorway. Fear was like a tangible thing that came between him and the bed. He wanted to turn and run down the stairs, but the impulse was momentary, to be beaten down. He forced himself to go across the room to the bed. He lifted the counterpane.

It was Jean Seyrac all right. The wry neck was twisted more grotesquely and round it was knotted a length of green picture cord.

Jean Seyrac was not going to Italy to-night.

A sudden sound of movement made Ross wheel from the body on the bed. The lime green curtain of the corner wardrobe was swinging back into place and in front of it stood Alvaro Parra.

"You shouldn't have come here, Mr. Barnes," Parra said in his nicely modulated Boston voice. "It was not wise of you. Not wise at all, I'm afraid."

Ross saw the muzzle of a small short-barrelled revolver, and the long, slender fingers of the musician's hand looked as if they understood this instrument. One of them brought a caressive touch to the trigger.

Chapter 16

Parra was very calm, just as he had been at their first meeting. He was not at all troubled by the rashness of Mr. Barnes. He deplored it for the sake of Mr. Barnes himself, as a duty, an obligation imposed by some consideration of politeness. The grey-green eyes were still incurious and quite without menace. The only venom was in the small revolver that pointed unwaveringly at the intruder's stomach.

"I thought I had created enough difficulty for you," Parra said. "I know your feeling for me is not very friendly, and now I'm afraid you will force me to aggravate it. I don't like to do that. I'm a reasonable man. I wish always to deal with reasonable men."

"Seyrac, I suppose, was unreasonable? And Kane?" The pistol might hold Ross from action but it could not control his anger. "What have you done with Ralph Peters? Where is he? If you've murdered him as you've murdered Seyrac, you'll pay for it."

It was absurd. It was futile. It was nothing more than the clamour of his anger.

"Mr. Barnes, I beg you to consider." Parra's free hand described a slight gesture of deprecation. "You place me under the distressing obligation of pointing out that you are being ill-mannered. It is unnecessary to shout at me or to indulge in crudities. The story of Seyrac is that he made himself unacceptable. It is not a gentlemanly act to talk about one's friends when an association is on a strictly confidential basis. As an intelligent man, you will appreciate that. You will also appreciate that your presence here supports the argument. Seyrac lost his nerve. He was a traitor in all but the deed."

"So he dies with a strangler's cord round his neck!"

"A mere symptom, Mr. Barnes." Parra brought a smile to his frank, pleasant face. "Seyrac, let us say, died of a too persuasive sister. His resistance was little, his knowledge was dangerous. You may count yourself fortunate that you were not a contact in the infectious stage. The disease is so frequently fatal."

"You damned thug! First Kane, and now this fellow!"

"It seems that you are determined to be rude." Parra shook his head slowly. "Kane's was altogether a different case, a grave error of social taste. He was trying to get ashore. We had treated him with every courtesy. We had even offered him privileges, but as a person he lacked the finer susceptibilities. He made a crude scene. He had to be restrained, with ropes. Unfortunately for himself, he broke free at a most inconvenient moment. We had just embarked a most important guest and the dinghy was riding astern. Kane seized the dinghy and started to row."

Parra changed his position slightly, coming forward a step.

"You may be disposed to excuse such impetuosity, Mr. Barnes. We could only look upon the act as unseemly. It placed us between the horns of a dilemma. If Kane reached the shore, the success of our peaceful cruise would be jeopardised. It was very necessary to correct the misdemeanour, because our programme was worked out on an exact consideration of time. We could not, you understand, risk an early alarm and the almost certain sequel of a night pursuit. Kane was stopped. Had I been on deck, I would have made an effort to recover the dinghy. Alas, I was fully occupied in the engine-room and quite unaware of the emergency. You will readily realise that we needed the dinghy. We had, in fact, to replace it with another boat, but I will spare you the details."

Parra was as proud of his plan and the execution of it as he was of his elegant periods. The weakness of the man came clearly to Ross through the hammering of his own confused thoughts. The thing to do was to let the fellow talk, even to play up to him in the hope that he might relax for a moment. It was the moment that Ross must seize, if it came, and he tried to prepare himself. Anger was no asset. His life depended on his getting complete control of himself, for he believed that Parra meant to kill him. Parra would shoot, if necessary. But Parra was cautious. He would avoid noise if he could. He preferred the silence of the green cord.

"You see how it is." Parra gestured again with his free hand. "Everything is planned beyond error, and you have been very unwise, Mr. Barnes, to entertain any thought of intervention. Even the police, with all their resources, are powerless. Inspector Laurent will never find us. We will hold Mr. Flavius as long as it suits us."

"I'm not interested in Flavius." Ross could speak quietly now. "I want to know what you have done with Ralph Peters."

"Of course. He is a very nice boy, Ralph Peters. If he behaves himself, nothing will happen to him."

"Where is he?"

Parra smiled. "If I tell you he is in your yacht, will you be any the wiser?"

The fellow was lying, but there was no sound of resentment in Ross's retort.

"He is not in the yacht."

"How do you know that?"

"She has been picked up, derelict. She's being towed in to Cannes."

"My congratulations, Mr. Barnes. I never had any wish to deprive you of your craft. To borrow her; that was all I ever intended. I hope you will find her intact."

"What have you done with the boy?"

"I imagine he must be with Mr. Flavius. That's a possibility, don't you think?"

Parra was quite amused. The pistol wavered. Ross decided that this was not the moment. He edged nearer, watching the trigger finger, weighing the chances of a desperate leap. One blow, correctly delivered, might knock the man out. It would have to be swift. So swift that Parra would have no time to shoot.

The conception was impossible. He amended it. So swift that Parra would not have time to level the gun and pull the trigger, and for that he must wait till the barrel was deflected. A gesture, a movement of the hand . . .

"You ask for too much information, Mr. Barnes," Parra said. "I would like a little from you, before we end this unfortunate interview. I want to know if Mr. Margolies has received any demand for ransom money."

"If he has, would he be likely to disclose it to me?" Ross answered.

Parra held his gaze with an intent, mind-probing stare. The pause lengthened, the stare became hypnotic, demanding. Outside, a car climbed the steep roadway in low gear, droning noisily. It seemed to go on past the entrance to the Rue Tunis. Then the noise stopped.

"You know about it," Parra asserted. "I wish to be informed, and I am not very patient to-night."

"If a demand has been made, you must have made it."

"Possibly you think that that is a reasonable assumption, but you are wrong, Mr. Barnes. I am not aware of what has been going on. You are aware. I do not have to be a mind-reader to see that. If you were more of a mind-reader yourself, you would not attempt to split hairs with me. Answer me, Mr. Barnes, or the consequences may be unfortunate for your nephew."

Ross answered him. If his gamble succeeded, it would not matter what he said. Parra would be delivered to the police, and the next move would be Laurent's.

"A hundred thousand Swiss francs!" Parra smiled one of his very nice smiles. "That is a small price indeed to put on the head of the fabulous Mr. Flavius. And the old trick with scissors and paste and newspapers! It is farcical! Don't you think so, Mr. Barnes?"

Ross could think only that here was the moment. In a gesture that might have been one of appeal, Parra moved the gun. More than this, his gaze shifted slightly as though something behind Ross had distracted him.

Bunching his knuckles for the blow, Ross sprang. He swung his fist up from the hip, but he was not quick enough.

Parra swayed. It was a flinching rather than a deliberate movement. Ross caught him on the side of the jaw, not on the vital point. The fellow staggered back and Ross followed swiftly, closing with him, grasping at the pistol hand. Parra was dazed, almost helpless. Ross bore him violently against the far wall and the revolver clattered on the bare floorboards. Then there was a shuffling sound behind him and he knew why Parra's gaze had shifted. Before he could turn to see the man who had come into the room, something as heavy as a monument and as hard as a battleship hit him behind the right ear.

He went down on his knees and pitched forward on his face. He was paralysed, blind with pain, but still conscious.

Another blow seemed to split his head into whirling particles. He heard a voice whispering from some far distant point, low, almost lost, yet giving venomous bite to the words. "Don't kill him, you fool! I want him alive!"

That was all.

Chapter 17

There were waves of partial sentience when he swung dizzily on some vast spinning disc. Then the edge would dip into a black gulf and he would know nothing. In one of the waves he was dragged across a rough floor, lilted, and carried down endless stairs. Later his head was throbbing like the engine of a car and he felt the coldness of a night. He was crushed down in a cramped space, and someone else was there, too, sprawling half under him. lie dipped into the gulf again, came out of it, dipped. The moments of dim apprehension became briefer. In one of them he reached out a hand and touched the cold face of a corpse. He tried to open his eyes, but the lids were too heavy, clamped down. The engine hummed, hummed, hummed . . .

After a long time he awoke to silence and found he could open his eyes. There were cold stars in the high sky and they swung past him in a slow dive, then up and back again, as if he were rocking in space. It took him several minutes to control the motion. Then he realised that he was lying on hard earth, and the dusty smell of it was in his nostrils.

It was difficult to think. More difficult to raise himself up and look round. He was aching all over and shivering with cold, and the pain in his head was a dynamo that sent out waves of sickness to hold him helpless. He let himself down and lay still for a while, waiting to get back some strength. When he raised himself again, he saw a mound or wall ahead of him. He got his back to it and leaned against it, trying to figure out where he could be.

A low moon was strong enough to light the scene, and slowly he made out some details. He was in a theatre, a small hill theatre of ancient design. He blinked. He couldn't believe that the thing was real. It was still too difficult to think because of the pain in his head. He could see, but could not reason. He was lying in front of the stage or platform in what might have been the orchestra. The terraced earth, once the tiers of seats, rose in a semi-circle before him, and above the farthest rim he could see the stars.

They were still now. There was that much gain.

He closed his eyes to rest. He felt a little better after a while, although there was no abatement of the pain in his head. He moved his limbs to get back some circulation. Hanging on to the low, broken wall, he pulled himself to his feet.

Next, he walked. At first he found it hard to keep a balance, but soon it was much easier, and then he could think again. He remembered that there were the ruins of a Roman theatre at Fréjus and concluded that this must be the place.

Off the main road and not far from Cannes.

When he got himself out into the open, he knew he must be right. He could see the sea, and below him were the lights of St.-Raphael.

Fifteen minutes later he was phoning Max from a hotel in Fréjus, and his first question was about Alicia Mars. Was she safe? Was she still there?

"Of course she's still here."

He was so relieved, the rest of it did not matter. He interrupted Max in the middle of a question.

"Don't let her out of your sight till I get back." That was the essential thing, all important. Another of Parra's hands might be waiting for her at the Villa Cerrito. "What did you say?" he added.

"When you failed to return, we went to the Rue Tunis to look for you," Max repeated. "The room was empty."

Empty?

He remembered then. Jean Seyrac had travelled with him in Parra's car. He remembered it all too clearly, his hand reaching out . . .

"I can't hear very well," he complained. "You're speaking too fast."

"We thought you had gone to the station with him. Did he catch the train all right?"

"Listen, Max!" The connection was bad and to shout was to increase the pain in his head. "Be careful what you say. I don't think you'd better tell the girl. Unless you prepare her somehow. Seyrac is dead. I was too late. I ran into trouble."

"What? Where arc you?"

"I'm all right. I've arranged for a car to pick me up. I'll be with you very soon."

It was three in the morning when he reached the flat. As soon as he saw Alicia Mars, he knew that Max had broken the news to her. She looked like death herself, but she had gained a measure of composure. She listened dry-eyed to the full story. A forlorn hope was finished, and, watching her, Ross had the idea that she must have been prepared for tragedy. At least some of the affection she had once had for her half-brother must have been replaced by a sense of duty to him in the last years. She was suffering, but she struggled to conceal it. She was solicitous for Ross. She had sent him into the danger. But Ross could think only of the danger that she might be in. If Parra believed that she knew too much, he would try to ensure her silence.

"I have no knowledge," she insisted. "I only wish I had, so that I could help you. Jean would say nothing to me. When I did find out about the kidnapping, he denied everything, until he became frightened. Then he said he would speak only to you."

"So now you have disappeared," Max decided. "Till to-morrow night you will stay here. Then I will take you to a place where you will be quite safe. You will write a letter to the Casino authorities and I will see that it is posted from Italy."

Chapter 18

In the morning *Roselle* was brought into the port and tied up at the *Albert-Édouard* jetty and placed under what amounted to arrest. Part of the jetty was closed to the public for a time. The swarm of reporters and special correspondents was matched numerically by detachments of police and detectives, and no one was allowed on board until a thorough examination, directed by Laurent, had been completed.

After that Ross was required to make another examination, with Laurent and Guizet on either side of him. The fingerprint experts and the official photographers had already had their picnic, and now the ears of the investigating body hung upon the comments of the owner.

It quickly became obvious that the pirates had treated the craft with respect. Everything was in place except the clothes and other effects that Ralph Peters had brought with him for the voyage, and there was not so much as a cigarette burn on the woodwork to indicate that unwanted guests had been on board.

In the saloon Laurent lowered his bulk into one of the arm-chairs.

"Well," he said, "we have found your vessel for you, Monsieur Barnes, but you do not seem very pleased."

"I will be pleased when you find my nephew for me," Ross told him. "That happens to be more important."

"And Monsieur Flavius. That, also, is important."

Ross was irritable. There was a complacence in the man from the Sûreté that might have got on his nerves even in better circumstances. This morning he was under too much strain, with all the burden of the information that he could not disclose without involving Alicia

110

Mars. And a splitting head for good measure. Of course he was relieved by the recovery of *Roselle*, but what did the fat monster expect him to do about it?

"I don't see that it's any great feat to pick up a derelict," he snarled. "Perhaps you're looking to the Navy people to do the rest of the job?"

Laurent, as far as it was possible for him to do so, shook his head deprecatorily, "It does not matter so long as the job is done. You must curb your impatience. You are almost as bad as Monsieur Margolies, who gives us no peace. To-day he is offering a reward of fifty thousand dollars. This afternoon it will be in all the papers. Scotland Yard has acquired a photograph of your nephew for us, He will appear on the placards with Monsieur Flavius."

"Fifty thousand dollars!"

"For Vincent Jacobson Flavius and Ralph Henry Peters, alive and safe. That may stimulate the navy." Laurent was being humorous. "I doubt if it will tempt any of the kidnappers, but of course one cannot tell. This is a peculiar case. Even in the financial markets, the effects present an enigma." He pulled a folded newspaper from a pocket of his jacket and thumped it. "Have you seen the reports from London and Paris this morning?"

"I'm no financial expert." Ross tempered his tone a little. He wondered what Laurent's reaction would be if he were told that another murder had been committed in the night.

"Pardon, I forget." Laurent closed his eyes as if he found the light of the Midi tiring. "Flavius and Margolies are the financial experts; those two and the Greeks of Operation Bouillabaisse. You are of the sea." He grunted. "I have a feeling that someone has been sailing very close to the wind, monsieur, but your nautical knowledge will not help me. We will keep to the land." He pushed the newspaper back into his pocket. "I have had another session with the woman Blieke. The waiter from Juan-les-Pins is sure that she met a dark-haired woman in his bar on the Rue Flaubert. Blieke continues to deny it. From you, Monsieur Barnes, I would like a fuller description of the woman you saw in the *Café des Lauriers*."

"I've already described her as fully as I can. I'm not very good at descriptions."

Now it was coming, but he was prepared for it.

"You identified her as Alicia Mars, the singer," Laurent reminded him.

"Inspector Guizet assures me I was mistaken."

"We are not so certain now. Alicia Mars, very curiously, has vanished. It is necessary to find out if she is the woman who met Madeleine Blieke in Juan-les-Pins. The Casino has provided a picture and we have shown it to our waiter, but he is unsure. Perhaps when we find the original, he will recognise her. We understand that you and Mr. Varenine made inquiries about her at the Casino last night. You are still convinced that she is the woman you saw with the wry-necked man?"

"I went to the Casino to find the answer to that." He met Laurent's gaze without flinching. "You can't expect me to be any more positive than your waiter, on the evidence of a photograph."

"And, of course, you failed to see the lady?"

Equivocation could best be served by another simple admission. Ross did not hesitate. "We asked for her address. We called, but she was not at home."

"So we will have to find her for you." Laurent attempted a smile. "Meanwhile, if you wish to remove any of your personal effects from your cabin you may do so. Inspector Guizet will take your receipt. I cannot allow you the run of the vessel just yet. If an insurance examination is necessary, we will grant facilities to your agents."

"I'd like my clothes. Also the money in my cash-box."

Ross knew that he must hide his fever of anxiety. If he rushed off, leaving his things, Laurent would be suspicious, yet the need to warn Max and Alicia Mars was urgent. It was impossible to know what was in Laurent's mind; how much he really suspected. A man from the Sûreté might knock on the door of the flat at any minute.

With Guizet at his elbow, Ross packed a suitcase and emptied his cash-box. Parra had been honest about pennies. Or he had failed to find the tin box under the bunk. Ross signed the required receipt and stepped on to the pier as if he had the whole day to kill. Newspapermen blockaded him, but all they wanted from him were two or three words about the recovered craft. When he had turned the corner of the Casino, he hurried along the few blocks to the États-Unis.

Max should have stayed at home to guard the girl, but Max had had to go out to the airport. He had persuaded Ross that there was no danger, because no one could know that Alicia Mars was in the flat. The concierge would think that she had departed in the night. In any case, Max had said, the concierge would admit no one.

But at that time there had been no thought that the police might be looking for their guest.

Ross tried to reassure himself. Even the suspicious Laurent would hardly imagine that the girl was concealed on the premises. But it was impossible to judge what Laurent might or might not suspect.

The fear that he was being followed made Ross look back. There was no one in sight. He walked on, turned again, waited. No shadow came from the Croisette.

Nerves. He was a case of nerves. A sense of calamity would not yield to reason.

The house door was closed, but this merely meant that the concierge was in the basement, doing the morning chores. Nobody could get in without a key.

Ross used the key that Max had given him. He fumed at the slowness of the automatic lift. He had the flat key ready in his hand. It had been impressed on Alicia Mars that she must not answer the door-bell or touch the telephone.

When he entered the flat, he called her name. He called twice, but she was not there. A note lay on the coffee-table in the living-room.

Dear Mr. Barnes, I have decided that I cannot put you and M. Varenine to any more trouble on my behalf. I do not know what the outcome of all this will be, but I have no right to ask you to take more risks. As it is, I shall always be grateful for what you have done. If I can think of any way to help you, I will let you know. – A.M.

His first impulse was to rush from the house and try to find her. She might have gone to the railway station where she had checked her things. She might have returned to the Villa Cerrito. She might have left the flat an hour ago. Or ten minutes ago. And by now it was possible that the police had detained her for questioning.

He hesitated. He thought of going to the Villa Cerrito, but a moment's reflection brought him the positive feeling that she would not he there. Unhindered, she would seek some place where she was not known, so the chances of his finding her were less than slender.

There was nothing he could do but wait for a call from Laurent and hope that it would come soon. In the hands of the police, she would be safe from Parra, and her safety had become his first anxiety.

He paced the carpet, he switched on the radio and switched it off. He stared into the street from the window and saw a postman passing towards the Rue d'Antibes.

That was something.

He went down in the lift to see if there were any letters. Four for Max and one for himself, from England. Back in the flat he opened his letter reluctantly. Eleanor was frantic about Ralph, demanding more news. He had written something each day. He could think of no more assurances to give her. No more lies.

More than ever disturbed, he put the letter aside. He must answer it some time, but not now. Perhaps, by the end of the day, he would find a glimmer of hope again.

He sat down with the morning papers and tried to figure out what Laurent had seen in the market reports, but it was no use. His thoughts kept returning to Alicia Mars.

The phone rang.

Already!

"Now, Mr. Barnes," Laurent would say, "if you'll come to headquarters, we will clear up the question of identity."

But it was Max who spoke to him, and Max exclaimed in dismay when he heard of the girl's flight.

"Laurent can't have anything against her," Ross argued. "She's intelligent enough to keep quiet. If they do find her, I'll have to say I never saw her before."

"That will be a great help," Max answered. "She wrote that letter to the Casino. By now it has been posted in Italy. If she is picked up in Cannes, what is she going to keep quiet about?"

"My god! I never thought . . ."

Max cut in on him. "I shouldn't have left her alone. You can't trust any woman."

"She was thinking about us."

"Never mind that. Meet me at the Rotonde at one o'clock. A press-agency man wants to talk to you. He's a friend of mine, Paul Jessel. I don't know what's it's about, but it's very important. He has some photographs he wants you to look at."

"Not Alicia again?"

"No. This is a new angle. He thinks he can break the whole business wide open. You can trust him, Ross. I want you to help him."

Chapter 19

Paul Jessel said nothing till the three of them were seated at a secluded table in a bay window overlooking the sea. Then he opened a large manilla envelope and spread a series of agency prints in front of Ross. They were all shots of a man who apparently did not like being photographed, and some of them were obviously taken under difficulties. The subject was hesitating on the steps of an exclusive hotel, hurrying across the Place Vendôme, waving the camera-man away in the foyer of a theatre, stepping into a large and expensive-looking car, shrinking behind a newspaper in the doorway of an air-liner.

Jessel was a swarthy little man, intense. He said: "Is that the character who hired this yacht from you?"

"Good heavens, no!" Ross looked up from the prints to stare at the newspaperman.

"You know the fellow?"

"I've seen him. I would say he was Merle-Florac."

"That's right," Jessel agreed. "Jean-Louis Merle-Florac. You're quite sure he's not the lad who posed as Margolies?"

"Positive. He was a different type altogether."

"You disappoint me, Mr. Barnes. You disappoint my chief."

"But how could you think that Merle-Florac would be mixed up in such a business?" Max wanted to know.

Mr. Jessel smiled a superior smile. "You'd be surprised! Though why you should be, I don't know. I've been investigating the great Merle-Florac. He interests me. He has all the charm of a slug under a stone.

I've been keeping tabs on his movements. Also on those of some of his hirelings. He was in London at the time your craft was chartered. He had been having conferences with Flavius. Later his pet accountant spent a holiday at Juan-les-Pins. Later still, the assistant to the personal secretary, a dish named Fournaise, who happens also to be his mistress, turned up in Nice. She was, in fact, working on her sun-tan along the *Baie des Anges* all the time Flavius was in Nice."

"Fournaise?" Ross was trying to think how and when he had heard the name.

Jessel pounced. "What do you know of her?"

Ross shook his head.

"Marie Fournaise," Jessel elaborated, still hopeful. "Personal spy, with quite a lot of the necessary equipment, if you like the type. Jet black hair and dark, burning eyes. Any offers?"

"No. I don't know anything about her."

Jessel sighed. "Maybe I'm all astray, but I still want to be convinced." He collected the photographs and pushed them back into the envelope. "I came here hoping for a bit of easy evidence. I guess we'll have to keep the story on ice."

"You're holding out on us," Max charged him. "What's at the back of it? You don't work up a story because Merle-Florac visits London and then sends this woman to the Riviera. It doesn't make sense."

"It might make sense of certain facts if we could find proof." Jessel turned the manilla envelope over and over in his hands. He was always moving his hands as if his strung-up nerves demanded some sort of action. "I'm not working up any story. I'm trying to fit a theory to the facts. Maybe I don't 'approach the problem as you do. You see, I'm the financial expert of my outfit."

The assertion had a familiar ring to Ross. He saw the fat hand of Chief-Inspector Laurent adjusting the thin lick of hair that straggled over a shining pate. He saw the small eyes peering from the creases in the suety face. He heard the echo of the wheezing voice. "Mr. Margolies, I am the expert of the Sûreté in cases involving finance."

Jessel said: "The facts are plain for anyone to read. Flavius is completing plans for a merger that will make him the controller of a vast international organisation. The list of the companies involved is ready. Agreements are about to be signed. Flavius holds all the strings, and Flavius is kidnapped. When the news flash hits the ticker-tapes, there is alarm in many quarters. On the first day, things are panicky. Rumours spread that the merger will fail. The market is shaky. Prices fall. Flavius has made himself a sort of Tsar, and, when the Tsar is missing, who knows what will happen."

"Another Ekaterinburg, perhaps?" Max was a shade sarcastic.

Jessel waved a hand impatiently. "Rumours multiply," he went on. "Prices fall. There is a little quiet buying on the kerb. Next day there is more quiet buying, here, there, everywhere. Not much, but it is organised. Not much, yet, because there is no general unloading. The morning brings a break in the Flavius dyke, but at the crucial moment a brave little Dutch boy shoves a hand in and plugs the hole. There is no more swirling on the face of the waters."

"You news boys are too picturesque," Max complained. "What does all that mean in plain talk?"

"There's a hell of a fight going on beneath the surface. One organisation is battling another. Someone's going to make a whacking big fortune. Someone else is going to go broke and buy some bullets for that old automatic that's rusting away in the bottom drawer of the desk. Whenever shares are offered, they're snatched up. Prices are rising. Meanwhile no one cares a two-penny damn about poor old Flavius. When it's all over, he'll be turned out to walk home, or he'll be washed up on the shingle with his throat cut."

"So Merle-Florac gets himself in on the merger, grabs the list, and turns his private thugs loose on Flavius?" Max was more than sceptical. "My dear Paul, you should write something for the Grand Guignol."

Jessel ignored the interruption. "One thing sticks out a mile. Treachery in the camp. Merle-Florac is one possibility. Margolies himself is another. Who could have worked it more easily? My own view is that something has gone wrong with the original plan. Maybe they just wanted to get Flavius out of the way for a few days, fake up a ransom demand to make it look good, buy up shares in the merger companies, and bring the old boy back to complete his deal. But the thing starts off with a case of murder, so what's more likely than that the thugs have got out of hand? In that case there'll be a real demand for ransom, and it won't be for pin money in Swiss francs. You needn't look so surprised, Mr. Barnes. Margolies told me, off the record. I saw him in Paris last night, fouled up in ticker tape and telegrams and cables."

"But he's here, in Cannes."

"He was in Paris all day yesterday. So was Merle-Florac. He had me thrown out of his hotel suite. Margolies agrees that the ransom is phoney."

Ross closed his eyes, but there was no glare of light for him. He was groping, recalling Parra's questions about the ransom demand. The shrewd Jessel had hit the mark. Something had gone wrong with the plan. The hired hand had taken charge. He still had Flavius. What was more important to Ross, he still had Ralph.

And in his groping, Ross remembered the scene at the *Hotel Alexandre*, in the office with the picture of the Gorges du Loup on the calendar.

Inspector Guizet was examining the agitated Miss Blieke, but Paul Jessel knew nothing about the agitation of Miss Blieke.

"Mr. Jessel," Ross said, "I'd like to see a photograph of Marie Fournaise."

"Give me your address." Jessel pressed the button of his ball-point pen. "I return to Paris to-night. If I can find anything, I'll send it to you."

Chapter 20

All the day Ross was held by the fear that Laurent might call upon him at any moment to identify Alicia Mars. He suffered, too, a recurrent dread that the body of Jean Seyrac might be found and the man's relationship to Alicia uncovered; but he told himself that Parra would not have gone to the trouble of removing Seyrac unless he meant to make sure of complete concealment. The motive might be to avoid the risk of inquiries in the Rue Tunis, to eliminate all traces of his crime, or to create uncertainty about the fate of Seyrac and throw doubt on any story that Ross might tell. Whatever it was, Parra would be left with the fear that Alicia Mars had dangerous information.

"The woman is a damned fool," Max complained. "Why couldn't she have stayed here till I got home? I had a safe place fixed up for her."

Ross said nothing.

"What makes it worse, she had some idea that she could still help us," Max went on, working himself into a dark fury. "I talked to her before I left her. That scoundrel of a brother was in trouble some time ago and had to go into hiding. In a craft of some sort."

"It doesn't matter, so long as she's safe," Ross answered in a dejection near misery.

"Doesn't matter!" Max came near shouting in his indignation. "Are you in love with her that you can say such a thing?"

"Don't be absurd!"

"A tug or a barge, she said. The fellow wrote to her several times. Like every other damned fool woman, she keeps every letter she gets. She keeps them, yes, but does she know where she puts them? She is distraught, she says, and can't think. Perhaps they are in the wardrobe-basket she left at the San Carlo. Perhaps they are in the valise with her programmes and press-cuttings. But the valise is with the American Express Company somewhere. Florence, maybe. Or did she have it sent on to the agents in Cannes?"

Ross shook his head. "I don't know what you're talking about."

"I'm telling you what she told me this morning." Max raised his arms in a Slavonic gesture that hinted at a despairing appeal to some invisible icon. "This brother and his accomplices hid themselves away in a tug or a barge. He did not tell her where, but there might be postmarks on the envelopes. The point is that they may have taken Flavius and the boy to the same spot."

"What?"

"I said to her, for God's sake, to find the envelopes. If we have to look for a tug or a barge, we must as least have a postmark. She said she would try to get hold of the valise. And what does she do? She panics and runs away, without so much as kissing you good-bye. Just like all these damned fool women."

Max had to have a drink before he could calm down.

"A tug," he said, "might be in any of the larger ports. A barge might take us along all the rivers and canals of France. That would be delightfully easy, especially as we couldn't tell one tug or barge from another."

"Then why worry about it? There's nothing more we can do. Perhaps, after all, Laurent will discover something."

"Call him up," Max urged. "See if you can discover Laurent."

The chief-inspector was not available. Ross spoke to Guizet. There was no news of Alicia Mars.

"Is Laurent doing anything about her?" Ross asked.

"He has been a little busy." Guizet side-stepped the question. "At the moment, he is in Hyères. There is possibly a clue. At least there is a curious fact. On the night your vessel was taken from Cannes, a rowing boat was stolen from a fisherman who lives near Hyères. As the kidnappers were without a dinghy, the report is significant, perhaps. It is not to be supposed that the kidnappers swam ashore when they deserted your craft, especially as Monsieur Flavius does not swim, inspector Laurent thought it necessary to investigate in person."

Significant? The course was westward. That was all. Fréjus, Hyères . . .

"Inspector Laurent is most anxious that you should confront Mademoiselle Mars. You will be informed as soon as she is located."

The formula had no sound of optimism. Guizet seemed annoyed about something.

Ross was trying to write some sort of letter to Eleanor when Margolies telephoned.

"I am just back from Paris," Margolies said. "I want to see you most urgently, Mr. Barnes. Do you think you could manage to come to the *Marinville* for a few minutes?"

The voice had the sound of a tired man, and, when Ross was taken up to the luxury suite of the Flavius party, he found a very tired man. Margolies was a wreck. He looked as if he had not slept for days. The face that had seemed fresh and young when Ross first saw it, was now so aged that the head of white hair no longer seemed incongruous. Overloaded bags dragged at the man's eyes and his whole person presented an effect of weariness.

Miss Blieke and her shorthand notebook were dismissed at once. Miss Blieke, too, as she retired, was a living expression of strain. She appeared ill. She glanced at Ross in a frightened manner and quickly looked away.

Margolies sifted a litter of papers on his desk and handed Ross a sheet of typewriting.

"First of all, I want you to read that, Mr. Barnes," he said, "I don't like to bring more trouble on you, but you will see that I have no choice."

The message had the appearance of being typed on the same machine as the letter that had awaited Ross in Marseilles. The only superscription was the day's date. It read:

The demand previously made on you was without authority. This, you will see, has a genuine endorsement. It must be followed in every detail and disclosed to no one but Mr. Barnes, who will receive from you, unopened, the enclosed instructions. You will hand to Mr. Barnes the hundred thousand Swiss francs which you have ready. You will then collect a further 500,000 Swiss francs in thousand-franc notes and wait for further instructions. If there is any failure, either by you or Mr. Barnes, the responsibility for what happens to Mr. Flavius and the boy Ralph Peters will be yours.

A scrawl penned in the margin was certainly an endorsement.

Caton — See that everything is done as ordered. This is the only hope for me and the boy. – Vince.

Margolies blinked his tired eyes. "That is unquestionably the handwriting of Mr. Flavius. Here is the enclosure."

Ross took the sealed envelope and opened it. Another typed sheet told him what he had to do and warned him, with a repetition of menaces, that he must say no word to anybody.

It was clear to him now, very clear, why Parra wanted him alive.

He folded the sheet lightly. "You are not to see this," he told Margolies.

The tired man nodded. "When will you want the money?"

"It has to be delivered to-morrow. If it's ready, and you will trust me, I'd better take it with me to-night. It will be safe in the flat."

"I have no alternative but to trust you, Mr. Barnes. I must follow instructions. I think I should tell you that I was suspicious of you at first. I was suspicious of everybody. But I had you investigated and I know you are reliable. We are in this business together now. If you need help, any sort of help, you can depend on me." Margolies unlocked a cupboard and took out a large brown-paper envelope. "The notes are in this," he added. "Let me know how you get on."

"In what way did the demand reach you?" Ross asked.

"By ordinary letter. It was posted in Nice, but I don't think that means anything." Margolies touched a bell button. "I'll have Delbert drive you to your door."

Chapter 21

In the morning the sun in a cloudless sky promised another fine day.

"I'm going for a walk in the country," Ross said.

Max looked curiously at the brown-paper envelope. "It is not your lunch you are carrying?"

"I can't tell you anything about it."

"All this mystery tells me enough." Max was anxious. "There will be danger."

"No."

"What makes you so sure?"

"I'll be making a second trip in a day or so."

"If you will let me know where and when the money is to be handed over, it may be possible to see something from the sky. I could track a car to its destination."

"I believe Ralph is alive and safe, Max. That's how he has to stay. Don't ask me any more questions, and don't try to follow me. I have to work to a plan and say nothing to anybody."

There was a timetable of a sort, as well as a plan. Ross observed every detail.

At eleven o'clock he found a taxi in front of the station and ordered the driver to take him up the Boulevard Carnot to Le Cannet. He paid the man off at the junction of the road to Grasse and started to walk along the highway, leaving Le Cannet behind him. When he had passed the last of the houses and come out on the shoulder of the hill, he could see a wide stretch of country with the road clearly visible until it curved round the conical elevation topped by the walled village of Mougins. The road ran on between acres of jasmine and fields of dark-trunked olives.

The terrain was admirably suited to the purpose, for the road could be kept under observation from a dozen points. Parra might believe in the strength the hostages gave him, but he was taking no chances. Even so, his agent for this test of faith was no doubt some expendable supernumerary. Perhaps he was waiting on the high hill of Mougins. Perhaps he was waiting in a car along the road that sprawled across the uplands from the direction of Antibes.

Ross tramped on at a steady pace towards Mougins. Far ahead of him, beyond his mark, he could see the town of Grasse perched high against the white and silver background of the Alpes Maritimes. A car or two raced towards Cannes. He passed a few houses. Then at the junction of roads below Mougins, he looked for a white stone on his right. It was a small cleft stone, his landmark. He pushed the envelope into some thick undergrowth behind it and walked on. He walked all the way to Mouans-Sartoux. He had a drink and a light meal, then waited for the train from Grasse to take him back to Cannes.

His job was finished.

Max arrived home early in the afternoon. He announced that he had been to the *Café des Lauriers* for lunch. "An abominable place," he commented. "I suffered, but I had an idea I would like to take a look at your friend the proprietor. By a curious coincidence, he was absent."

"Where is the curious coincidence?" Ross asked.

Max went on as if he had not heard. "I inquired about him and was told he was out on business. I began to wonder if his business had taken him into the country. He turned up about two-thirty. Would that be all right for time?"

"I don't know. Did you think I might have come across him? I saw nobody. What made you go to the café?"

"It interests me. It is so peculiarly close to the Rue Tunis, and somebody must have been keeping an eye on Jean Seyrac. And on his visitors. I do hope that fool of a girl has not run into trouble. If we do not hear from her very soon, I think we should go to your friend Laurent with the whole story."

"Why should we hear from her?" Ross was bitter about it.

"I have a feeling that if she is free she is looking for those old letters from her brother."

Chapter 22

At six o'clock Ross went to his old friend Laurent with a news photograph showing Marie Fournaise boarding a train with Merle-Florac. The picture of the noble financier was a little indistinct. That of the woman was excellent. It showed a handsome face with wide-set eyes and prominent cheekbones, a large and slightly aquiline nose and full lips. It was the sort of face that even a moronic waiter should readily remember.

The expert from the Sûreté seemed a little dejected. He scowled and grunted.

"You are not bringing me any information," he said. "I am fully aware that Marie Fournaise was late for dinner on the night in question. That has been explained. She was sent to a pharmacy with a prescription for Merle-Florac himself."

"It has also been explained that Mademoiselle Bheke went for a walk. Your waiter says he saw her with a dark woman. This woman, Fournaise, is dark."

"So is the Queen of Ethiopia, monsieur. I think you should realise that these matters of detection are best left in the hands of the professional."

"All I ask is that you should show the photograph to the waiter in the Rue Flaubert. It is at least something to do while you are trying to find Miss Mars."

"Miss Mars has been found." Laurent fixed his small eyes on Ross in the slightly disdainful stare of the infallible professional. "She has written to the Casino from Italy. We are, at the moment, in touch with the Italian police."

"But the waiter is uncertain about her picture. He may be positive about this one. It will not take us long to go to Juan-les-Pins."

Laurent meditated a moment, grunted, then heaved himself out of his chair. "All right," he agreed. "There is no harm in seeing what the waiter has to say. You shall come with me."

There were not many customers in the Bar Baraban.

Laurent isolated the waiter and showed him the picture.

The man responded with an excited exclamation. "But that is the woman," he cried. "Undoubtedly that is the woman. Now you will believe me when I say that she was here with the red-haired one."

On the way back to Cannes, Laurent said: "I will go straight to the *Hotel Marinville*. The chauffeur will take you to your flat."

Ross objected. "I want to hear what the girl says."

Laurent was silent till they were crossing the base of the Croisette. "Very well," he agreed at last. "You have given me a point and you may help me with the girl. There is always a moment when pressure is needed. It is psychological. But I beg of you, please, you will be silent till the moment. This is entirely a matter for the professional."

He was familiar with the arrangements at the hotel and known by now to the staff. He led the way to the lift and demanded the Flavius suite.

Miss Blieke, coming to the door, flinched visibly when she saw Laurent. However reluctant she might be to admit him, she had learned that he was not to be put off. Ross followed him into the room where he had seen Margolies the previous night.

"If you want Mr. Margolies, he isn't here," the girl said hopefully.

"That is, perhaps, unfortunate." Laurent was disarmingly amiable. "There are one or two things I would like to discuss with him."

"He had to go to Marseilles. He will not be back before eight."

Laurent looked at his watch. "Then we will have a little chat while we wait. You know Monsieur Barnes. May we sit down?"

She assented with all the readiness of one who sees rack and thumbscrews ahead.

"I'm very busy," she said. "You'll have to excuse me."

"In a moment." Laurent's fat fingers fished for the photograph of Marie Fournaise in its envelope. "There is another little picture I want you to see."

"If it is Alicia Mars again, I have told you that I do not know her. I have told you again and again that there was no one with me in the bar."

Already the edge of hysteria was in her voice. Laurent paused deliberately, watching her.

At last he said: "All I want you to tell me is the truth. Look at this picture."

She reached for the print with an unsteady hand. She held it close to her in an effort to control the trembling, but when she saw the face she was clearly shocked. For a moment she was without any control, shrinking from an accusation as though Laurent had said: "That is the woman you met." She rocked back in her chair, closing her eyes tightly. Laurent waited. At last she looked at him,

"Why do you show me a picture of Marie Fournaise?" she asked in a small voice.

It was then that Laurent said it. "She is the one you met in the Bar Baraban when you had your cassis. That is why."

"I met no one. Marie Fournaise was not there."

"You will find it difficult to deny the evidence of the waiter. He recognised the photograph at once. He is ready to swear to it." He turned to Ross. "Am I right, Monsieur Barnes?"

This then was his moment. The psychology was crude, a mere matter of numbers.

"You are right," Ross responded sharply. "The waiter is quite sure."

"You see, mademoiselle." Laurent held out a hand to take back the photograph. "You can no longer deny it. The waiter makes a positive statement. You left the bar with Marie Fournaise. You sent a message to Monsieur Flavius. He walked from the *Hotel Alexandre* in answer to that message. A few minutes later he was in the hands of the kidnappers."

"No, no!" Her voice rose to a scream. "I had nothing to do with it."

"You are going to tell me, perhaps, that it was Marie Fournaise who sent the note?"

"No."

"But you left the bar together. You admit that?"

She was rigid in the chair now. She closed her eyes as though against a fierce glare of light. Laurent repeated his words and waited. He was good at waiting.

"I admit nothing."

Laurent got on to his feet. "Very well, mademoiselle. You will come along with me to headquarters."

The girl, with an involuntary movement, pushed her chair back. "You can't arrest me" she cried. "You can't do it! You can't."

"Try to keep calm, mademoiselle. I ask you to come with me. We have your depositions in the dossier. We will go over them carefully. We will find out where you went wrong."

"No!" She was frantic. "You can't take me away. I haven't done anything wrong. What I did, I did under orders."

Laurent made an inarticulate sound, a sound of triumph. It had the staccato suddenness of fingers snapped together. This was the break. Miss Blieke wept. Laurent was at her side, not to console her, but to insist on an answer to the pertinent question.

"So you did meet Marie Fournaise?"

An affirmative came jerkily between sobs. The room door opened and Margolies walked in, back from Marseilles. Margolies, still driving himself against weariness, was in a state of nerves himself.

"What the hell goes on now?" he demanded, and pitched at Laurent in anger. "I have already protested about your treatment of the girl. I'd like to know why you persist in asking her a lot of useless questions."

"She has confessed." Laurent gave his narrow collar a tug and straightened his white tie.

"Confessed what?" The note of incredulity in Margolies' voice suggested he thought that Laurent must be mad, but he was shaken by the simple statement that followed. He grasped the girl's shoulder. "Is this true, Mady?" he asked sharply.

This time the affirmative was a drawn-out wail.

"She says she acted under orders," Laurent explained. "Whose order's? Were they yours, Monsieur Margolies?"

"I don't know what you're talking about. Mady, for heaven's sake stop crying. Who gave you orders?"

"Mr. Flavius. He – he told me I was not to say anything." She fumbled for a handkerchief and blew her nose. "Not to a living soul."

This was heresy or treason to Margolies. Something unbelievable. His grip on the girl's shoulder caused her to wince, but she must have taken some assurance from it. The few sobs that followed were the last.

"What am I to do, Caton?" she pleaded. "He made me promise. Not even to you, he said."

"That's past," Margolies decided. "You should have told me at once. You must tell us everything now."

She was relieved. The whole thing had been a heavy burden, wearing her down. Now that Caton was ready to take the responsibility, she could not get the story out fast enough.

It began in Nice, where Marie Fournaise was on vacation, waiting to join Merle-Florac in Juan-les-Pins. She had met Marie a year before and they had become friends of a sort. And Marie made her the confidante of all her troubles. Marie was very unhappy. Merle-Florac had treated her badly. If she could get another job, she would leave him flat.

Mady had a lot of spare time in Nice, so she saw Marie nearly every day. They bathed together, dined, went to the films. Mr. Flavius saw them together. Mr. Flavius was quite observant. He remembered Marie, because there had been some preliminary conferences with Merle-Florac the year before. "If she ever talks about her boss," Mr. Flavius said, "just listen to what she says."

This was not a nice situation. A girl had to be loyal to her employer. She also had to be loyal to her friend, even if the friend was a bit of a fool and sometimes rather a bore. Mady listened, but reported nothing. There was really nothing to report. It was just that Merle-Florac was a brute and as mean as a miser. Poor Marie had to work for a pittance and yet she was expected to dress like a couturier's model. And what

Merle-Florac wanted for a few francs was nobody's business.

After several more days, Mr. Flavius had a heart-to-heart with Mady. He had heard rumours about the financial affairs of Merle-Florac. He wasn't satisfied that Merle-Florac was a good risk for the merger, and here was a heaven-sent opportunity to do a little pumping. He instructed Mady what to say, the sort of questions to ask. Mady still hadn't liked it, but just about then Marie began to throw out hints. There was a lot she could let out if she cared to open her mouth. And the next day she followed this up with a more suggestive variation. There was no limit to what she could spill, if it were worth her while.

"She said she had seen the books," Miss Blieke added.

"She often had to make entries in the private ledger. Naturally, I told Mr. Flavius."

"And he fell for it, the damned old fool!" Margolies exploded. "Couldn't he see that you were being led? It serves him right. By heaven, it does. If he'd said only a word to me . . ."

"One moment, please!" Laurent interrupted him. "Go on, mademoiselle."

Miss Blieke was too shocked by Margolies's outburst to go on. "Caton!" she protested.

Caton was in a fury that would not be stayed. "For years I've run this goddamn business for him, keeping his pants up, buttoning his suspenders, and he has to do this behind my back. He can fry in his own stew. Fry!"

Laurent was a monument of calmness. "Go on, mademoiselle."

"I had to take an offer to Marie." The girl hesitated as if she saw that what she had to say was going to bring trouble for her. "Mr. Flavius would give her a job in New York if she could supply him with figures. She agreed, and arranged to meet me at the Bar Baraban the night we arrived in Juan-les-Pins. She said it was too dangerous for us to have any contact at the hotel. When I met her she said she wouldn't have the figures till the next day. She also wanted to be sure that Mr. Flavius would pay for her to fly to New York before Merle-Florac could suspect her. We didn't stay long in the bar. We walked along the front for a while. Then she said I had better start back to the hotel ahead of her. When I went upstairs after dinner, there was no one in the sitting-room, so I thought Mr. Flavius had gone to bed."

"And you didn't suspect anything next morning?" Margolies howled the question at her. "Why didn't you tell the police as soon as they came?"

"I couldn't think. I was frightened. It didn't seem possible that Marie could have had anything to do with it. When I heard about the note, I began to wonder, but Mr. Flavius had been very strict about the order to say nothing. Then I got more and more frightened. I thought I would be accused of sending the note to get him out of the hotel."

"Look at me, mademoiselle," Laurent demanded. "Do you say that you did not write any sort of note to Monsieur Flavius?"

"I swear I didn't."

"Supposing you did? Supposing you had written that Marie Fournaise had the figures and wanted him to come for them? Would he have come?"

"Most likely, yes."

"If Marie Fournaise had sent him a note?"

"I don't know. I don't think so."

"Did you ever write any letters to her?"

"Yes. After we met last year, we exchanged letters. I wrote to her from New York."

Margolies broke in, his wrath little abated. "So they had all they needed to fix up a forged note. And all their elaborate plans depended on whether he would swallow the bait."

Laurent grunted. "No doubt they had an alternative. More dangerous, perhaps. More violent. This was the easy way, and the victim did, in fact, swallow the bait. If he hadn't, they would have lured him into some corner somewhere. Perhaps into a car on some pretext. The timing would have allowed for that much margin. If we assume that Merle-Florac was behind the business, he would have had resources."

"Assume?" Margolies looked as if he were in danger of a seizure. "Who could have been behind it but that damned double-crossing scoundrel? Go after him, man! Arrest him, before he can get away."

"It is a little difficult without proof."

"Look! He's been fighting me in the market ever since it happened. That was the motive; hold up the merger operation by getting Flavius out of the way, then buy, buy, buy. Buy merger shares all along the line, buy up everything with the name of Flavius in it. I suspected the Merle-Florac interests from the start. Now I'm certain. He was out to make millions, but I've beaten him. He didn't know I had a full power of attorney. He didn't know that I was the real Flavius, ready to throw in the last cent against him. He's finished now. You've got him tied hand and foot. Kidnapping, murder. . ."

Laurent interrupted the excited flow with a surprisingly swift gesture for him.

"We cannot go into a court of law with theories," he objected; "any more than we can find the prisoners of the plot by sticking a pin in a map."

"Get Merle-Florac and you'll soon know where Flavius is."

"No." Laurent shook his head. "This thing has slipped from the hands of the instigator. He has lost control to the criminals he employed for his purpose. If he had not, Monsieur Flavius would have been released by now. I am not for nothing the expert of the Sûreté in affairs of finance. I have been watching the markets; without your inside knowledge, but with enough of my own. By last night the fight was lost, yet Monsieur Flavius is still held. At any moment now, you may expect a real demand for ransom."

Margolies jerked his head back nervously, as if the reminder had come as a jolt. "I have already had it." He spoke more soberly and glanced at Ross. "A first instalment was paid today."

Laurent picked up that glance. "By Monsieur Barnes?" he asked. "This is interesting. He, too, has a hostage in the enemy camp."

"I am not going to discuss it. Neither is Barnes."

"Just one question, if you please. There was no contact?"

"The demand came by mail."

Laurent's gaze moved to Ross.

"There was no contact," Ross said.

"An instalment," Laurent mused. "This will go on and on. As long as the golden eggs are laid, the goose will be kept alive . . . Mr. Margolies, I will use your telephone. It is a direct line?"

"Yes."

Laurent called the operator. "Interurban communication, please." The others watched him as he hung ponderously over the instrument giving instructions for an urgent official call to the Sûreté Nationale. When he got through he demanded Inspector Saval. He grunted, then spoke sharply.

"Saval? Jean-Louis Merle-Florac will be at his usual hotel, no doubt. All his movements are to be watched. Also, you will locate Marie Fournaise, one of his secretaries. She is to be kept under close surveillance. Be ready to bring her in for questioning as soon as I reach Paris . . . Yes. I will see you in the morning. That is all."

"That is all," he repeated when he put down the receiver. "I must be on my way at once. I will be back in Cannes to-morrow night if I can catch a plane."

Ross stayed for a word with Margolies. He walked home, making a circuit to take a look at *Roselle*. She was safe, guarded by a man in uniform. She would stay there at her berth until she was delivered back to him. In a matter of days, perhaps, but he found no pleasure in the thought. There would be no Tiny Kane to start up the engines; no Ralph to give the brass work a wipe or hang out a shirt on a rigged line.

He turned away hastily. When he opened the door of the flat in the Rue des États-Unis, he realised that Max had a visitor. He hesitated, but Max called to him eagerly to come in.

The visitor was Alicia Mars.

Chapter 23

The gladness he had in seeing her was mingled with alarm that she was here. The first thought he had was that one of Parra's men might have seen her, might be watching, hidden somewhere in the street below.

"You shouldn't have come here," Ross said.

"I had to come," she answered. "By now the police will believe that I am in Italy."

"It's not the police. They're no longer interested."

He began to tell her why, but Max interrupted him.

"Alicia has found the letters from her brother."

Ross stared questioningly.

"They were in an old suitcase at the Villa Cerrito," the girl explained. "My friend Peggy Segal brought it to me."

"Why did you come here?" His first concern was for her. "It would have been safer to telephone."

"I was anxious not to delay. I wanted you to see the postmarks. One of them is clear enough. It is Béziers. The other I could not make out."

"Unquestionably it is Lunel," Max asserted. "It is smudged. The first letter is very indistinct, but I am sure of the last two."

Ross saw that he had a large-scale map spread out on his desk. He took the two torn envelopes that Max offered him. The date, as well as the name, was clear on the one posted in Béziers - a little more than a year ago.

A little more than a year ago Jean Seyrac, fearing that the police might be after him, had gone to a hiding-place provided by Parra.

"So the argument is good," Max said. "Parra may well have Flavius and your nephew stowed away in the same place. It is a bolt-hole he has kept available. Possibly it has served him more than once, and it has never been discovered."

"You will read about it in one of the letters," Alicia explained. "The other one does not matter. Let me show you."

She took the flimsy sheets of note-paper from under the map and found the place for Ross to read. He watched the movement of her hands as she came to him. Then she was at his side, very close to him, and he had in that moment the realisation that she had become more important to him than anything else. There was a pause when he stared at the letter without reading, when he felt only his anxiety for her and a very desperate need to keep her safe. Then he read the words scrawled in pencil:

I'm sorry I got into the scrape, but it was not my fault really. Anyway, you don't have to worry about me. I must not tell you where I am but I'm safe. There are two of us and we have an old disused wine barge all to ourselves and we have made it fairly comfortable. I think the timbers must have sprung and it was not worth salvaging. As it is we have water laid on — or laid under us — for it washes right up against the floor. If we lifted a few boards we would have a swimming pool. And for scenery there is a nice marsh. Well, I must close now, kid. My pal is waiting to mail this. I know I am just a good-for-nothing heel, but if you want to cheer me up some time, drop a line poste restante Montpellier and it will reach me eventually. The new name is Jean Seyrac. Rather imposing, don't you think? Keep up the good work. You'll make the Metropolitan one of these days. Love and best wishes. — Jay.

Ross looked up from the letter to meet the gaze of the girl's clear blue eyes. She had no more tears for Jean Seyrac. If she had wept for him, it must have been for a part of him that was lost years ago, beyond retrieving. She was a little lost herself now. Ross held her gaze.

"So we have three points: Béziers, Montpellier, Lunel." The practical Max broke in on them, and the map rustled crisply as he smoothed it out. "If we take a line from Lunel to Béziers, or, say, the mouth of the Orb, we've quite a stretch of coast to cover west of the Rhône delta. It's likely country for a wine barge. For hundreds of them. It's all made up of marshes, canals, étangs. See! Here's the canal running down from Lunel."

He traced the line on the map with his forefinger.

"It connects up with this other canal here. This big pool is the Mauguio étang. Here's the airport, close to Montpellier. That's useful. And the canal goes all the way down to Sète through this chain of pools. Sète is the big wine port for the Languedoc."

Max looked up, frowning. "All we have to do is find a waterlogged wreck somewhere near a marsh. First pick your marsh, then look for a barge in some shallow backwater. And how are we going to know it's the right barge, supposing we do spot something?"

Hope died in Ross when he looked at the map.

"You can try," the girl urged.

"And pray for a sign, perhaps?" Max bent over the map. "Flavius on deck, playing Monopoly with Parra."

"We'd better turn the clue over to Laurent," Ross suggested. "He has the resources to handle it. He can investigate every waterlogged barge he finds."

"And he'll know the right one because it will be empty. Parra will move house at the first hint of police activity along the étangs." He looked up from the map. "Tomorrow we'll try. At least we might pinpoint a few hulks that look likely. There are two or three airfields scattered over the country - one between Agde and Béziers, another near Lézignan-Corbières – so they'll be used to planes in the sky. We'll be able to take a close look without stirring up a panic."

The forlorn hope might succeed. Ross was moved by a renewed eagerness in his friend.

"I'll never be able to repay you for all this," he said.

"I'm doing it for the reward." Max grinned. "If we bank those Flavius dollars, the three of us will share them. Alicia will be able to buy herself an opera house. Now we'd better see about getting her home. I'll go down and make sure that the street is safe. Parra hasn't had any of his boys on the job up to now. I've been keeping my eyes wide open. If I don't come back in ten minutes, you can make a start. And walk. I'll be following, just to be sure. Alicia tells me it isn't far."

It was a small pension in a cul-de-sac off the Boulevard d'Italie.

They were silent till they had crossed the railway line. Then Ross asked her: "What will you do now?"

She hesitated. "There is my career. I have engagements in Italy next month. I shall go back."

"At once?"

"No."

"It would be safer for you."

"Perhaps I am in no danger. I shall stay till this is over. If there is anything I can do to help, I must do it." She hesitated again. "Will you let me know what happens to morrow?"

"Of course." They were at the gateway of the house. "I would come here, but it may not be wise."

"I'll telephone."

"Is there anything I can do for you?"

"Nothing."

Max was waiting for Ross at the entry of the cul-de-sac.

"It is all right," he announced. "There was no sign of any shadow. She should be safe enough if she is careful."

He was still thinking of the girl as they walked back along the Rue d'Antibes.

"It would be better if she were across the frontier, but perhaps we will soon see the end of it. I feel hopeful about to-morrow. If we find the barge, it should be easy for Laurent."

"It will not be easy for us," Ross answered him.

"Except that I have a presentiment. I won some money last night. Our task is certainly difficult, but the omens are good. I have a flight fixed for ten in the morning. That will not take long. As soon as I get rid of the customers, we will start off. You had better go to bed. You look as if you need a lot of sleep. I will visit the Casino for a while. I am playing a new system and it is working well. When luck runs with you, you must keep in step."

Chapter 24

Marseilles was below them in the morning sun with Notre-Dame-de-la-Garde reaching up towards them from its high hill and the Old Port gleaming like a slot of silver. The pattern of the docks spun away from under them and the Château d'If was a vanishing dot in the sea behind.

Then the coast spread before them a crazy jumble of pools and streams and marshes, traversed by the regular lines of canals. They saw the Rhône flowing into the sea through its many mouths. They were over the watery reaches of the Camargue, crossing the great nature reserve of the Etang de Vaccarès.

Their landmark of Montpellier was in sight. From Aigues-Mortes they swung up towards Lunel, then banked for their first run over the stretch of étangs and waterways that Max had marked on the map.

There were barges under way on the canals, waiting in ports, moored in backwaters. Max took the plane down beyond Narbonne Plage, made a wide turn inland, and ran over the course again. Up and down and round about they went many times, diving and climbing and diving again so that any curious observer might conclude that they were joy-riding or practising manoeuvres. Certainly they must have given the impression that there was little method in their madness.

Max's hopefulness of the night was dissipated before their take-off. Luck had deserted him at the Casino, his new system had failed him, the omens had turned rancid. By the time they had landed at the airport outside Montpellier to refuel and get some lunch, he had plunged to a zero of pessimism.

"One might as well try to find a pea in the Sahara," he complained.

There were several barges that fulfilled the conditions hinted at by Jean Seyrac, stationary, with marshy surroundings, and from the air you could not tell whether they were moored or grounded. And how were they going to distinguish one from another?

Ross looked glumly at the dots he had pencilled on the map.

"The thing to do is to hire a launch," he decided. "Then we can explore thoroughly. We could be on a boating holiday."

"And how would we earn our keep till Doomsday?"

It was not: quite as bad as that, but Ross made no protest. Instead, he studied the map.

"If the barge was anywhere near Lunel when Seyrac was on it, he would scarcely have given Montpellier as a poste restante address," he argued. "That would be placing it too near home. I think we ought to concentrate on the area lower down the coast, near Béziers."

The complexity of canals and winding pools ended in the great Thau Basin between Sète and Agde. Below Agde the lay-out was much simpler, with a relatively straight coastline, but the section between the Midi Canal and the Aude had its quota of rivers and creeks, of pools and marshes.

"There are lonelier spots round here," Ross pointed out, with a finger on the map. "Likelier spots, far away from the main canal traffic."

"Far away from Lunel, too," Max grumbled.

"Forget Lunel. That letter was probably posted by someone on the way out, to Aries or Marseilles. The Béziers postmark seems more significant to me."

"All right, if that's how you feel." Max drank coffee. "Let's get up in the air again. It's too gloomy down here."

Ross had marked two or three barges in the area, and Max, taking a south-westerly course, picked up the Hérault River at Pézenas and followed it to the coast. Then they flew along the creeks and over the marshes and pools in the hope of seeing some sign that would define their quarry. Perhaps the sinister figure of a guard, Max suggested. A pirate with a pistol in his belt, or an assassin on a bicycle, pedalling home across a marsh with a full shopping basket. Max had revived a little, but his humour was sour.

Sometimes a figure waved cheerfully from a deck and then Ross would put a cross against the corresponding dot on his map, for such an amiable gesture was scarcely likely to come from any of Parra's hands.

For another hour they flew over the hunting ground. There were other planes up, practising manoeuvres, so now their own plane would be less conspicuous in its goings and comings. Max made wide sweeps round Agde to aid deception, but always he was soon back over the marshes, and Ross picked up barge after barge with his binoculars and searched the deck of each of them.

One more run, and inevitably they must head for home.

Suddenly Ross saw something.

"Look!" he shouted. "The Arab's nightshirt! That barge in the backwater to the left of the creek. Come round, Max! Come round! But keep well away. They mustn't suspect us."

Max climbed and swooped, and Ross swung his binoculars on to the object.

There it was. The sign. A white shirt fluttered against the dark deck of the barge. It was pegged by the shoulders to the rigged clothes-line and each sleeve was turned twice round the line and held by a peg at the cuff, just as Tiny Kane would have done it. The deck revealed no other sign of occupation, but Ross knew that Ralph Peters was on that barge.

His hand was shaking as he drew a circle round the appropriate dot on his map.

"Keep going," he urged Max. "Work all the way up to Sète. If they get the idea they've been spotted, they'll bolt before we can act."

Max did the job thoroughly. He was far to the north of Lunel before he turned in the direction of Cannes.

Chapter 25

Chief-Inspector Laurent seemed sceptical, or he was in a bad mood, lie stared at the map, a new copy with only one barge marked on it. He stared at Ross, then at the map again.

"But it is fantastic," he said.

"What is fantastic?"

"The assumption. You see a shirt from the air and come here and tell me that Flavius and the boy are on a barge! What were you and Varenine doing, flying over that part of the country?"

"I've told you. Varenine wished to make a pleasure flight. I went with him."

"And when you are over the étangs, you see this shirt, just by accident. Aren't you allowing your imagination to run away with you?"

The question was undoubtedly justified, but Ross could not disclose the reason for the flight. That would have involved the story of Jean Seyrac, and he was determined to keep Alicia Mars out of it. Bald and unconvincing as his statement might be, Laurent had to take it or leave it.

Ross argued : "I wasn't allowing my imagination to run away with me when I brought you the photograph of Marie Fournaise last night."

Laurent grunted. He was certainly in a bad mood, and mention of Marie Fournaise aggravated it. His urgent visit to Paris had resulted in nothing but frustration. The Sûreté had failed to produce the woman. She was, it was said, on a week-end visit to her parents in Normandy, but inquiries made by the Rouen police had brought the information that she had not arrived, though her parents were expecting her.

The inspector had called on Merle-Florac at his hotel, and Jean-Louis had treated him as if he were an offending menial. Jean-Louis was a very important person. The failure of the Sûreté to find and rescue his dear friend Vincent Flavius had jeopardised his patriotic work. If a fumbling police could not do a better job and do it quickly, a great financial advantage might be lost to France.

Laurent had to curb a wrath that rumbled in him like lava in a burning mountain. A man of his weight has to be careful when poised on egg-shells. Merle-Florac had no lava in him. He was glacial.

"How should I know anything about the movements of Mademoiselle Fournaise?" he asked. "The inquiries of your department have been answered by my secretary, who granted the application of the young woman for a few days' leave. I have nothing to do with the minor arrangements of my staff. It is no business of mine whether she does or does not go to Rouen. Nor can it be any business of yours. I know nothing about her relations with Mademoiselle Blieke. I am not acquainted with Mademoiselle Blieke. It is not possible that any member of my staff could throw any light on the doings of a stenographer employed by Monsieur Flavius. If the girl has conveyed such a suggestion to you, she is obviously lying. If you wish to question Mademoiselle Fournaise, she will no doubt agree to see you when she returns to her duties on Tuesday. But that is a matter which is no concern of mine. If I am subjected to any further annoyance, I will be forced to make a complaint to my friend the Minister. That is all, monsieur."

It was not quite nil. Laurent had at once gone to the Minister himself. An order had been issued for the arrest of Marie Fournaise and the instruction to keep Merle-Florac under observation was doubly underlined. Nothing more could be done about the great man until the girl was brought in, unless he made a false step. Laurent had been quite cryptic about Madeleine Blieke's evidence and had said no word about his waiter witness, but he had given Merle-Florac enough to worry about.

Now, back in Cannes, Laurent was doing some worrying of his own, and the persistence of Ross in these amateur efforts was like an irritant on sore flesh.

"I admit your help, Monsieur Barnes, in the matter of Marie Fournaise," he said. "But this shirt is quite something else. Do you really expect me to raid the barge on such evidence?"

"Yes." Ross was without hesitation. "There is no imagination about it. The evidence could not be stronger."

"A shirt and nothing else. You do not identify the shirt itself. You base everything on the way it was pegged to the line. The argument is, no doubt, that the boy is permitted to do odd jobs about the barge. That is reasonable. You do not suggest that he saw the plane approaching, concluded you were in it, and contrived a deliberate signal? That would be a little too much."

"And it is neither here nor there. I've already told you why he would hang out a shirt in that way."

"You've also told me that nobody else would."

"It would be an incredible coincidence."

"I must disabuse you, monsieur. I have an ancient female relative who always twists the sleeves of shirts round the line on a windy washing day."

Ross was shaken. It could be true. For all he knew the trick might be a familiar one to all the boatmen along the Rhône. Yet it might be that Laurent, obstinate in incredulity, was romancing to give support to his objection.

Laurent waited. When Ross said nothing, he added: "So, you see, it is not wise to be so positive."

But the momentary doubt was gone. Ross was positive.

"Are you going to do anything about it?" he demanded with a note of challenge in his voice.

"I cannot answer you at once." Laurent's fat hands gripped the desk in front of him as if he were about to rise. "If you will leave the map, I will consider."

"I hope you appreciate that we cannot afford to lose time. Flavius and the boy may be moved at any moment . . ."

"I appreciate everything, including your reasonable impatience. All I can tell you is that inquiries will be made. Then we will decide if any action is justifiable. Meanwhile, you will refrain from meddling. This is not a case for amateurs."

Max was waiting at the flat to hear the news, and Ross was furious as he delivered it, railing against Laurent. "If that baboon and his monkeys start nosing round, they'll scare Parra into flight. The job should be done to-morrow at latest."

Max agreed. "It would be a good day. Saturday afternoon is a suitable time for a fishing party." He pulled Ross's marked map from the desk and studied it. "Most likely we could hire a craft in 'Agde."

"I can't believe that Laurent will ignore it. How can he?" Ross moved about restlessly. He started to pour himself a drink, then decided against it. "Did anyone ring me while I was out?"

"What?" The map rustled as Max looked up. "Heavens, yes, I'm glad you mentioned it. Margolies wanted to talk to you."

Margolies did not interest him. He told himself he should have fixed a time for Alicia to call. She might have phoned before they got back from the flight.

"More ransom trouble, I expect," Max added.

"What?"

"Margolies. He decided to come here to see you as soon as he has finished his homework. You can make some more seltzer and give him a high-ball. It's too late to put down a new carpet." Max rose and stretched. "I'll step round to the Casino for an hour. They missed a couple of mille notes when they went through me last night."

"Wait!" Ross suddenly saw Margolies in life size. "You'll stay here till he comes," he insisted. "We'll tell him everything and make him get some action. Laurent will have to listen to him."

"First we have to convince Margolies. Frankly, Ross, I don't know that I'm convinced myself. All the same, I'd like to know the answer, and only the barge can supply it."

"Stick to that. You'll have to support me."

Max was fretful, almost as restless as Ross while they waited.

When he came, Margolies was in a hurry. "I've a plane waiting to take me to Paris. I thought I'd better look in on my way to the airport, Mr. Barnes. If we could have a few minutes ..."

Ross introduced Max. Margolies was inclined to frown at the thought of another confidant, but found that he had to accept the situation.

"A new note has come by mail," he reported. "The money is to be delivered on Monday morning. Here are your instructions, sealed again, as you see."

Ross took the envelope but did not open it.

"I'm worried, Barnes," Margolies confessed. "There's a third demand, another instalment. It's just as Laurent warned: as long as I keep on handing out money, there'll be no end to it. Frankly I don't know what to do. This time there's no okay from Flavius. I feel that I ought to turn the whole thing over to Laurent. Before I dash off, you'd better see what you have to do on Monday. The money will be ready for you. I'm putting a letter in with it, giving them an ultimatum."

"Perhaps it will not be necessary." Ross pulled a chair forward. "Sit down, Mr. Margolies. We've something to tell you."

"I must be on my way. I've work to do in Paris before the Bourse opens to-morrow morning. Whatever's in your mind will have to wait."

"This can't wait. Sit down and listen. We've found out where Flavius is."

Margolies opened his mouth, but nothing came out of it. He sat down. He was silent till Ross had finished his story and Max had confirmed it, and Max was now emphatic in confirmation.

"Without a doubt," he said, "Ralph Peters is on that barge. You can make up your own mind where Flavius is."

"Perhaps you can persuade Laurent to take immediate action," Ross added. "If he won't move, Max and I will. We're making a fishing trip to-morrow afternoon. We're going to get on board that barge."

"Let me use your telephone."

Margolies was on his feet and reaching for the instrument. His call was not for the police, but for the *Marinville*. He spoke to Miss Blieke.

"Get the airport and cancel that plane. Are you listening? Put a call through at once to Paris. Tell Kerr he'll have to carry on without me. He knows what to do. If anything unforeseen comes up, tell him to use his judgment. Tell him I can't get away. Tell him anything."

He slammed the receiver down. He was excited, but his brain worked coolly, already calculating chances.

"How many men will they have on that barge?" he asked Ross.

"Not many. I don't think there are many of them in it."

"Why? What makes you say that?"

"The man who tricked me over the charter was very eager to know about my crew. He knew there would be only three of us in the vessel. Then he made quite a plot to get me out of the way on the night of our arrival in Cannes so that he'd have only Kane and the boy to face. He had helpers on shore, of course, but my idea is that he had no more than two or three men with him when he went on board."

Max approved. "There's another point in favour. They had to plan to get their prisoners to the barge by dinghy. When Kane ran off with it, they were forced to steal another small boat. I don't think there would have been more than three of them."

"They might have made two trips to the barge." Margolies was not objecting. He wished to look at all the possibilities.

Ross shook his head. "They wouldn't have risked two trips. They could have run pretty close inshore, piled into the boat and turned *Roselle* loose with engines running. I think Max is right. There wouldn't have been more than three of them."

"But they could have put a dozen men on the barge since," Margolies argued. "Some of their shore helpers."

"They wouldn't need many to hold an old man and a boy. A crowd would attract attention and be difficult to feed."

"What does it matter?" Max asked. "Three or three dozen, Laurent can marshal all the men he needs. The thing is to get him to act."

"But you and Barnes were going to board that barge without help?"

"Not entirely. I had it in mind to take along a couple of hard-knuckled lads from the port." Max grinned. "It's rather a pity we have to hand over to the police."

"We don't have to." Margolies developed a sudden warmth of voice as he went on. "If you two are willing, we'll go into it without the law. I know the obstinacy of that Laurent fellow. He'll want finger-prints and birth-certificates before he moves, and maybe an Act of Parliament. We can't have this bungled. By the time the police get organised, those crooks may have the wind up."

"You could bring pressure and insist on immediate action." Ross felt a last twinge of caution in his fear for Ralph. "Unless you don't trust Laurent?"

"I don't like him. I don't like the way he treated Mady Blieke. He may be well-meaning. He may be efficient, according to the book, but it's not my style of book. I'm afraid. That's the whole truth. I'm afraid this chance may be missed, and I'd never forgive myself. With a bunch of police closing in on that barge, anything might happen. We, at any rate, could get close enough to look things over."

Margolies took up the map, glanced at it, and threw it down.

"All right, Mr. Varenine," he went on. "You get your lads from the port. I've kept my own knuckles pretty hard and Delbert is an expert. That will make six of us. I'll charter your plane for the trip if you can carry us."

Max shook his head. "Too many for me."

"Then forget it. I'll hire something and we'll have a car from Montpellier meet us when we land. We'll take off about seven. That will give us plenty of time to find the sort of craft we need at Agde. If you'll have your party ready by six, I'll call here for you."

Margolies was in a hurry again, but now his destination was the *Marinville*. At the flat door he turned to Max.

"Get the toughest hands you know," he urged, "and don't stint the danger money. Flavius will meet all expenses."

Max went with him to the lift. They were both in the same mood, like a couple of schoolboys. Ross had been carried along in the discussion, but now he had misgivings. He went to the window and looked out. The big Bentley was at the kerb with Delbert in attendance. Max came back.

"Why the look of gloom?" he asked. "Are you going to blow cold, now that everything is fixed?"

"I'm worried about the girl," Ross answered. "She promised to call me up to-night. It's getting quite late."

"So it's Alicia!" Max grinned. "I thought it might be the barge."

"The barge isn't altogether out of it." Ross was testy.

"What if Parra has picked her up? What if she has been made to tell about those post-marks?"

"Don't work yourself into a state of nerves. Go to her pension and satisfy yourself. Or phone her?"

"I promised to wait. I'll give her a while longer."

"Just as you like, but you'd better make sure. I'm bound for the port. I can't delay."

Max was a little uneasy himself, but he made light of it. Left alone, Ross tried to concentrate on the plan for the next day, but he could think only of Alicia Mars.

Finally he looked up the number of the pension and jotted it down. Then, as he reached for the instrument, the bell rang and he heard her voice.

The explanation was quite commonplace. She had called twice, and each time the line had been engaged. Then she had decided to visit her friends at the Villa Cerrito, which was quite close.

"You fool.'" It flashed from him as if he had the right to be angry with her. "You shouldn't have gone there. Where are you now?"

"Back at the pension. I'm sorry. I didn't think there was any harm in it."

He apologised, although she had not protested. "Don't leave the place again till you hear from me," he begged. Then he spoke to her in guarded terms, as if he were afraid someone might be tapping the line. "I may not be home till very late to-morrow," he said. "Perhaps not till Sunday. I'll have good news for you. I'm sure of it."

He was sure of it in that moment, but now she was full of alarm. "You've done enough," she urged. "You mustn't run any risk."

"There's nothing to be afraid of," he assured her. "I'll call you as soon as it's over."

"Please," she said. "At once, please."

He put down the receiver and poured himself a drink. The plan took shape quickly then, and he saw all the details clearly. He saw snags and mishaps and ways to counter them. And he laughed when he thought of Laurent. The great man from the Sûreté was going to be taught a lesson. Now, if only Max would come back, they could discuss the whole picnic, but Max, by this time, was probably at the Casino, losing more money.

The phone rang again.

"Barnes? Margolies here. I've just had news from Paris. Marie Fournaise has got away, on a plane bound for Brazil. Merle-Florac committed suicide three hours ago. I guess there was nothing else for him to do."

"Nothing else?" Ross could not take it in. "Do you mean to say that Laurent's visit frightened him into suicide?"

"I don't know. The woman was in flight already. He may have meant to join her in Brazil, but probably we'll never learn the truth of it. His secretary has made a full statement. Merle-Florac was finished, ruined. His affairs have been in a hopeless mess for a year or more. He was counting on this merger gamble to pull him through. I can see now how desperate he was. He had to be, to start this crazy kidnapping. When trading closed to-day, it was the end. He went up to the roof of his hotel and jumped off."

Chapter 26

Early on Saturday afternoon a small, clumsy-looking launch stuttered down the Hérault from Agde, took the sea with a slight lurch, and turned the point to follow the curving coastline southward. It was a patched contraption, overdue for a coat of paint. The corroded brasswork, the scarred and stained forward deck, the torn and faded canopy over the well, were clamant signals of age and neglect. The exhaust gave out a high-pitched popping that suggested the tinny complaint of an over-stretched kettle-drum. The engine, too, had a tinny sound, but it could still kick a few knots behind it, and the veteran craft made good progress.

A trio in the restricted area of the well, where the engine took up a good deal of space, suggested a bourgeois family on a happy excursion. At the tiller, a full-bearded man in a white yachting cap had the appearance of a shopkeeper on holiday, and the character who lolled on the seat at his side might have been his wife. The third member of the visible party was a robust young fellow in a striped shirt and white duck slacks who was busy laying out some fishing tackle on the deck. The son and heir, perhaps? There was no resemblance to the other two in the cut of his jib, but that happens in the best-behaved families.

Madame, who was watching the engine closely, leaned forward and made some adjustment. She was dressed comfortably for the voyage in roomy scarlet slacks and a more than roomy blue silk shirt, and, though obviously competent when it came to engines, she looked emphatically feminine. Almost oppressively feminine. The emphasis was laid on regardless, with rouge and lipstick, and her fine head of henna had a permanent wave that was positively tidal.

Satisfied with the engine, she peered at the coastline ahead, then studied a folded map.

"Bring her over a bit," she instructed the man at the tiller. "It's the third opening past the big inlet."

"Okay, Max." The voice of Delbert came from the bearded face.

Max spoke in French to the young fellow on the deck. "We're getting close, Pierre. Any questions?"

"No questions, Mama." Pierre grinned. "I know what to do, If there's any argument, just leave it to me."

"Good." Max stretched and called into the cabin. "Now's the time for a breath of air. You'll be a long time below, once we run into that backwater."

Margolies squeezed himself through the cabin hatchway, mopping his face. Ross followed him. A third man remained in the cubby-hole.

In less than another hour the launch had entered the creek.

It was easy-going between level banks for the first quarter-mile. Then there was marsh, with the waterlogged land laid out on both sides of them in a pattern of sedgy hummocks and twisting channels lined by thick growths of tall rushes.

Pierre went forward and sat astride the bows with a boat-hook ready in case of trouble, but the creek was still a wide though winding channel defined by a sluggish current, and the hand at the tiller was in no difficulty.

Max stood on the deck, gazing ahead across the marsh.

"Do you see anything?" Delbert asked.

"No." Max rose on his toes but had to shake his head. "The hummocks are too tall. There couldn't be a better place to hide. There's nothing to be seen, except from the air."

The reeds and rushes closed in on them, narrowing the channel of the creek.

"Port," Pierre called suddenly, but Delbert had already marked the bend.

A tall hillock, another bend, and they emerged upon the waters of a wide étang.

Max caught the drone of a plane above the low-speed panting of the launch. It was coming, perhaps, from the field between Béziers and Agde. A small private kite, a two-seater. It hummed slowly over at five hundred feet and disappeared in the direction of Narbonne.

The launch was halfway across the big pool before Max caught a glimpse of the barge through a veiling of bamboos. He called the news to Ross and Margolies and warned them to get back inside the cabin.

"If they have a look-out, we're sighted by now," he said.

Pierre used his boathook as the launch scraped bottom and jibbed. They swung into the channel again, and Delbert watched the current more carefully. The neck of an empty wine-bottle bobbed towards him.

The thin feathery tops of the bamboos nodded in a light breeze. They were close now, and there was more marsh beyond then. The launch went on between low banks, and in another minute the barge was clearly visible.

It lay on the far edge of a pool or backwater to the left of the creek. It was grounded on a fairly even keel, settled in mud, and there no doubt it would stay until it fell to pieces. Three shirts flapped lazily on the clothes-line, but they were pegged in an orthodox way, not in the manner of Kane's mythical Arab.

The two-seater plane came over again, heading up the coast towards Agde.

Ross peered from the hatchway.

"For heaven's sake touch up your face, Max/" he urged. "You look like the dame in a pantomime."

"Stay below," Max warned him. "We're in full sight."

They passed the entry to the backwater. Max was lolling on the seat again. He stopped the engine, produced a compact from a pocket of his slacks, and powdered his nose. The launch swung in towards the bank and Pierre dropped the kedge overboard.

Pierre sang gaily and danced a few steps on the deck. There was chatter. A hamper appeared, and from it food and wine. Such a pleasant bourgeois picnic! Madame shifted her position so that the canopy would guard her complexion from the hot sun. Pierre assembled the fishing-rods.

In the cabin Ross, Margolies and the extra hand, a muscular young man named Jules, peered through the curtained windows at the barge, now separated from them by the low bank and thirty or forty yards of water.

It was a small barge with a squat deck-house aft, and the laundry on the line was still the only evidence that it was occupied. From a point amidships a gang-plank, reaching to a tufted knoll, gave access to a path that picked a sinuous way across the marsh towards firm land in the distance.

Margolies was dubious. "There's nothing unusual about those shirts," he pointed out. "Anyway, if our friends are on board, why should they show any washing at all? Anyone with any sense would try to keep the thing looking like an abandoned wreck."

"They're sure of themselves. They've used this hide-out for years." Ross was arguing against his own doubt as well as that of Margolies. "Nobody comes this way. In any case, it's safer for them to be open with the local people round about. They have to come and go to get provisions. They've probably pitched some tale that they've bought the wreck. If it were known to be abandoned, there would be visitors. Youngsters would swarm all over it, tearing it to pieces."

"Maybe. Are you quite sure of that shirt you saw from the air?"

"Let's wait," Ross suggested. "That's what we're here for."

They had not long to wait. The door of the deck-house opened and a man stepped out. Ross caught hold of Margolies' arm and gripped tightly.

The man closed the deck-house door, came forward, and stared across the water at the launch.

He was Parra.

Chapter 27

For a moment or two he seemed undecided. He started back towards the deck-house, but wheeled suddenly and stepped down the gang-plank to the knoll. Then he began to make his way towards the creek, stepping or leaping from knoll to knoll till he reached the bank alongside the launch. It looked dangerous, though obviously he knew his marsh, and, even in the most strained moment of his chameleon-like progress, he never failed to convey an impression of elegance and an ease of athletic co-ordination. And he looked more like the fastidious owner of a neighbouring chateau, the grand seigneur himself, than the opportunist squatter of a waterlogged hulk.

He was dressed for the part in beautifully cut tweeds. The knee-high rubber boots were a little incongruous, but the inevitable concession to local conditions.

He was amiable. His frank, pleasant face had a smiling warmth. Only the grey-green eyes did not smile. His greeting was, perhaps, a shade on the seigneurial side, but you understood that his good breeding enabled him to consider sympathetically the human problems of the bourgeoisie. There was a tacit acknowledgment of the rights of man, and more especially of humble shopkeepers on an angling picnic. Possibly he was himself a practitioner of the gentle art.

In the circumstances, the response of Pierre was a little grudging, a trifle surly, but this may have been according to the book. Monsieur, too, was rather stiff. Madame contented herself with a shy smile and a furtive fingering of her henna-dressed tresses.

"I'm afraid you have come to a bad place for your sport," the amiable seigneur remarked. "I have never known anyone catch a fish in that creek."

"No?" Pierre shrugged. "Perhaps they do not use the right bait."

Monsieur cast his line and watched his float carefully.

"I have no wish to discourage you," the seigneur said. "But I very much fear you are wasting your time."

"It is our time," Pierre told him. "Fish or no fish, we like it here." And he cast his own line.

Madame smiled shyly. What could she do about it? These men of hers wished for peace and quiet. So much was in her smile. She fluttered her eyelids and pulled down the bottoms of her scarlet slacks more becomingly.

"Do you live in the barge?" Pierre inquired.

"Sometimes."

"It is a strange place to live."

"Yes. I suppose it would seem so to you." The seigneur smiled condescendingly. "I find it very much to my liking."

"You are a hermit, perhaps?"

"Of a sort. I am a writer. I come here to work in solitude."

"I thought you might be hiding from the police." Pierre was really a gauche young man. "It would be a good place for that job. Have I read any of your books?"

"That, I am afraid, is a question I cannot answer." The seigneur was modest. "I am not very well known."

"I like a good detective story myself. I don't suppose you write that sort of thing?"

"Alas, no. I incline more to economics."

"Everyone to his taste." Pierre reeled in and had a look at his bait. "You must find it lonely, all by yourself on a barge in the middle of a marsh. But perhaps your wife comes with you to do the washing?"

"Not quite. I bring my man with me."

"Just the two of you on that barge, like Crusoe and Friday?"

"Yes. Do you find it so very peculiar?"

"No." Pierre shrugged. "It wouldn't suit me, that's all. I suppose the living is cheap. Did you have to pay much for the barge?"

"Not a great deal." The seigneur's smile had become a little steely. "Perhaps I should leave you to get on with your fishing. From my own experience, it is hopeless. Nevertheless, I wish you the best of luck."

Madame, who had been watching Monsieur's float, turned to give the visitor a shy smile in farewell and to observe his nimble performance in retreat.

Delbert spoke quietly to the three in the cabin. "Two of them! Did you hear that? And there are six of us? What are we waiting for?"

"Carry on with the programme," Ross ordered. "There may be more than two of them. That fellow was putting up a tale."

"If we knock him off, the others will scuttle."

This time Max said no. "We follow the plan. Get on with the fishing." He hauled his wrist-watch from his slacks and put it on the seat beside him. "We move in thirty minutes from now."

Ross and Margolies watched through the cabin windows. When he reached the barge, Parra was joined by a man from the deck-house, and they talked for a while. Then both of them went into the deck-house, and a moment later Parra reappeared with a Spanish guitar under his arm. He sat on a deck-chair, tuned his guitar, and played, and at last Ross knew the use he made of those fine, beautifully cared-for fingers. They capered on the fretted neck and plucked the strings with virtuoso skill in the intricate and traditional pieces of Spain, the true music of the instrument, and across the water came the rhythms of the jota, the malaguena, the zapateado, with dazzling improvisations in between. And all the time the musician watched the launch, ready, perhaps, to hail the landing of a tiddler with a burst of sardonic chords.

But there were no fish. Not even tiddlers.

The last of the thirty minutes ticked away, and Max, repairing his face once more, gave orders.

"Get the anchor up, Delbert. Pierre, you start the engine."

Max pocketed his watch and laid a heavy, foot-long spanner in its place on the seat.

They moved and turned in the stream. Max lolled conspicuously, but as they passed out of sight behind a slight rise in the bank, he snapped forward and did something to the engine. Then he was back on his seat again and the engine began to splutter and miss. Delbert swung the tiller and the launch took a curving course through the entry into the backwater and swung over close to the barge, just as the engine gave up with a final asthmatic cough.

Parra put down his guitar and came to the side.

The brash Pierre got in the first word. "Thanks for the music. You were right about the fish. We thought we'd have a try in here. We can't go home without a bite. No supper."

Parra was not smiling any more. For a moment he seemed a little perplexed.

"You can't fish in here," he said harshly.

"Who says we can't?" Pierre snapped back. "Maybe you own the place?"

"Yes, I do. At least I pay for privacy," Parra spoke more mildly, obviously trying to restrain himself. "I think I have a right to be left in peace, if only as a matter of good manners."

"And we've a right to fish."

The launch edged nearer to the barge as Delbert played with the tiller. Parra's companion came from the deck-house to join him. He was a burly, ugly-looking customer.

Parra said: "All right, my friend. There are no fish, but, if you will not listen to me, you must go ahead. Just one word of warning. It's getting late, and if you don't cross the étang before the light fails, you will be in trouble. It is not easy to keep to the stream unless you know the way. Take my advice, and try the creek on the seaward side. You are more likely to catch something there."

Pierre scratched his head, turning to Delbert. "Perhaps he's right, Papa. Anyway, we don't want to stay where we are not wanted. Shall I start her up?"

"Oui," Delbert grunted. "Oui, oui, oui."

The tension relaxed. Everybody was pleased. But the engine would not start. Pierre laboured, swinging the wheel.

Cough, splutter, silence. He tried again. The result was the same.

"Name of a name of a dog!" he swore. "What's the matter with the thing? It worked beautifully all the day."

Delbert shrugged and grunted. Max shrugged and smiled. Pierre swore and laboured.

"So we'll be here all night," he cried. "All night without fish! I don't know what's wrong with the misbegotten contraption. The man told me to swing the wheel. That's all. Swing the wheel, he says." He looked across at Parra. "Do you know anything about these engines?"

It was the bait. Parra knew all about engines. In the cabin, Ross and Margolies and Jules waited, tensely expectant.

Parra spoke to his companion, then called to Pierre. "Throw a line and we'll haul you alongside. There's plenty of water."

Ross, ready to spring through the hatchway, reached back to touch Margolies on the arm.

Pierre threw the mooring line from the deck and leaned out to grasp the side of the barge as Parra hauled. In the well, Delbert performed a similar office. Max smiled sweetly at the Samaritan who was so ready to help them get away. There was less than eighteen inches between the deck levels as the smaller craft snuggled in. Parra made the line fast and stepped on to the foredeck beside Pierre.

"I'll see what I can do," he said. "Is there fuel in the tank?"

"Plenty," Pierre answered. "Perhaps the feed is choked. It is very good of you. I am afraid I was a little rude."

"It is nothing. It is important for you to be off before night comes."

Parra jumped into the well. Max moved to make room for him. Parra stooped, bending over the engine. Max grasped the wrench. His vivid blue shirt-sleeve flashed as his arm rose and fell, and Parra sprawled helplessly across the engine. Pierre sprang on to the barge to grab the astonished spectator of the outrage. Delbert hit the higher deck with a more acrobatic vault and rushed to assist. The burly one struck out, yelling for help. Pierre took a knock that sent him reeling, and the hard-fisted Delbert missed his mark with a driving left. Nevertheless it all looked absurdly easy to Ross as he and the others swarmed on to the barge.

It was not so easy.

Help poured from the deck-house. The man in the lead tossed a hand of playing-cards into the air and leaped at Ross. There were five newcomers, so, with Parra knocked out, the numbers were even, but the boarders had gained some advantage by surprise, for the card-players, suddenly disturbed, had answered the alarm with no weapons but their fists.

Ross met his man with a blow that rocked him, but was sent to the deck by the next fellow. Then, in a vicious scramble, the contenders swayed back and forth across the barge. Ross was on his feet again and doing damage, but the defenders were tough. Jules, armed with a heavy stick, was picked up by a bull-necked Hercules and hurled at Max before he could get in a blow, and Max, crashing painfully on his right wrist, lost his useful spanner. He also lost his red wig.

Margolies had mustered pistols for Ross and Delbert and himself, but it had been agreed that there should be no shooting unless the enemy started it. Now, with the struggle going so badly, he hauled out a short-barrelled revolver with the idea that a threat might change the situation.

"Get back! "he shouted. "Up with your hands!" But the bull-necked one rushed at him, roaring contempt, dashed the weapon from his grasp, and sent him toppling. Ross, at the same instant, tried a flying tackle on the fearless assailant, but it would have taken three men to hold the fellow. Dragging Ross with him, he went back into the fray, and merely shook his head when an upper-cut from a berserk Delbert took him on the jaw.

Ross, hurled off, closed with another opponent. Max flashed past, his face smeared with lipstick and blood. Jules was swinging his fists like a windmill in a gale, Pierre hit out with his stick, Delbert got his gun from his hip and used the butt. The Hercules still stood, though his mates tumbled and rolled round him. Then a shot cracked dully through the shouting, and the sound of it went echoing over the pool. Another shot, and the unlucky Jules dropped to the deck, groaning.

"Get back!" Ross yelled, "Get cover!"

There was cover of a sort: the coaming of a hatch, the housing of what had been a winch, and a squat, rusty bollard. The boarding party dived for what was the nearest to each of them before they saw the menace of the muzzle held at deck level.

Parra had come back to consciousness. Parra had pulled himself up in the well of the launch, and, shielded by the side of the barge, had intervened with a sniper's shot.

"To the deck-house," he ordered his crew. "Get your guns, imbeciles!"

Splinters flew close to his head as Delbert fired from behind the bollard. Parra snapped a shot back at him.

Jules lay groaning on the deck, and close to him was the revolver that Margolies had lost, irretrievable.

Covered by the coaming of the hatch, Ross levelled an automatic at the door of the deck-house.

"Keep Parra busy," he called Delbert. "I'll look after the others."

At the first movement in the doorway, he fired, meaning to wing the man, but the bullet smacked into the woodwork, wide.

He calculated. Parra had a revolver and had fired three shots. Three more and he would be defenceless. Even if he had more bullets in his pocket, he would not be given time to re-load.

It would be dangerous. There were two windows in the deck-house. A defective automatic might hold the enemy in the coop, but they could still cover the deck from the windows.

Ross edged forward an inch and a bullet from Parra hummed past his pistol hand.

Delbert fired, and Parra replied with a quick one-two.

That was it. Six.

Max let out a yell and rose from behind the winch in his war-paint. The windows spat bullets at him and Max gave a different kind of yell. He was hit, but not disabled.

Ross aimed at the starboard window and squeezed his trigger. Parra fired again.

So he had two guns, and, if he had the bullets, he could go on re-loading indefinitely.

It was stalemate, if not defeat. Stalemate, and no way to break it.

But it was broken, and quickly. The throbbing of an engine came from the creek, and the swift crescendo of sound told of a speed-boat pushed to its utmost.

Parra shouted a panic command and Ross heard the tautdrum sputter of the launch's exhaust. Then the mooring rope hung slack over the barge's side, and the launch was under way.

The bull-necked man came from the deck-house shooting wildly, and the others, streaming out behind him, dashed for the landward side of the barge and sprang overboard. Delbert and Ross fired together and Hercules was down at last, sprawling on the deck.

Ross and his companions rose from cover in time to see Parra leap from the launch and start running along the bank of the creek. The other men were strung out along the path across the marsh, going as fast as their legs would carry them, and the cause of it all, the urgent speed-boat, came curving into the backwater, leaving a tumbling wake behind it.

Then uniformed police, rushing across the deck of the barge, started a chase, and Ross saw similar figures start up from the meadow beyond the marsh and advance without haste to head off the fugitives. The trap was complete.

Ross hastened to the deck-house shouting the name of Ralph. He heard a muffled reply from below. A stairway, a door with a key to it, and then he had Ralph in a bear's hug. He was quite oblivious of the great Vincent J. Flavius till he heard a voice say: "Well, Caton, this is quite smart of you. I hope you managed all right in my absence."

Chief-Inspector Laurent stood on the deck like an over-fat Napoleon, watching the final phase of the battle of the marsh.

His brow was heavy with anger as he turned lumberingly to glare at Ross.

"How often do I have to tell you, Monsieur Barnes, that such things should be left to professionals?" He waved a heavy hand in a gesture of rejection. "These amateur theatricals . . ."

Chapter 28

The casualties suffered by the boarding party were not serious. Max had had his neck grazed. Jules had taken his bullet in the left shoulder, but the hurt was of little consequence. In addition, there were a few bruises, a few sore heads, some broken knuckles. On the other side, Hercules, with a wounded thigh, was in worse case, but no one had any sympathy for Hercules. His friends were too busy worrying over their own misfortunes.

Except for the discomfort of life on board the barge, Flavius and Ralph had not come off so badly. The indomitable good manners of their host, that singular arbiter of social taste had seen to that. Indeed, Ross was to gather that Ralph, after the terrifying experience of the first night, had rather enjoyed the adventure. He had been given more liberty than Flavius, had helped with the meals and the general chores, and so had found opportunity to twist the sleeves of a shirt round a clothesline.

"I knew you would take it as a signal," he told Ross. "I tried it two or three times when planes were over. Yesterday I somehow felt that it was you up there. I thought Kane would be with you. When he got away in the dinghy, Mr. Flavius and I were sure he would give the alarm at once."

"He gave the alarm," Ross answered, and left it at that for the moment.

"Ralph was wonderful all through," Mr. Flavius put in eagerly. "I have great plans for him. When I am in London, I will talk to his parents. In future, it will be all right for Ralph. And it will be all right for you, Mr. Barnes."

The great man was in a munificent mood, determined to reward all his rescuers. The difficulty, it seemed, would be to restrain him from overdoing it.

Everybody on the side of the law was happy. Even Laurent expressed satisfaction when he added up his bag of prisoners, he tackled Parra at once, on the deck of the barge, but for once Parra was disposed to waver from his own high standard of behaviour, overcome, perhaps, by the vulgarity of Laurent's interrogative style.

"You had better hire a spiritualist and get in touch with Merle-Florac," he suggested. "Possibly he will answer your questions."

"So you admit that Merle-Florac was the instigator?"

"Yes, if the admission is necessary. Does it comfort you?"

"And this preposterous plan of chartering a craft in England was his?"

"Why preposterous?"

"Why?" Laurent grunted in his best manner. "You go to the ridiculous length of impersonating Mr. Margolies, you have the *Roselle* brought all the way to Cannes, when all you had to do was pick up a craft anywhere along the coast at little expense. Instead, you throw away sums of money to produce this fantastic situation."

"It was Merle-Florac's money."

"And you made yourself the executor of his imbecile invention?"

"Do you call it that?" Parra descended to contempt. "I see you are puzzled. So far as I am concerned, you may go on being puzzled. You and all the rest of your dull-witted plodders at the Sûreté. Give me my guitar, and have the courtesy to leave me alone."

Laurent had more success with some of the other prisoners, and especially with one who was eager to make things easier for himself by giving all the help he could. Then, when the preliminary statements were put together, the plan was seen to have been less illogical than Laurent had supposed.

The charter of *Roselle* had been Parra's own inspiration. Merle-Florac had sent him to London to keep an eye on the movements of Flavius and Margolies during their brief stay in England, and the advertisement in The Times had offered him an easy solution to a pressing problem. It had indeed been intended to pick up a craft somewhere along the Riviera, but the right kind of craft was not so easy to find. So many were privately owned; so many had already been hired. And a speedy vessel was essential to the plan. There were also dangers in the local situation. Merle-Florac had, of course, to be kept well out of it, Parra and his accomplices were not unknown along the coast. Awkward questions might be asked.

But here, offered in a London newspaper, was the very thing they were looking for. And available at a French Riviera port! If the business could be transacted in London, everything would be quite safe. Parra asked the chartering agent for details. Merle-Florac gave his approval, and his devious mind at once suggested embellishments to the original plot. Parra was to impersonate Margolies and let the owner think that Flavius himself was responsible for the charter.

Then, when Parra saw the craft, he realised, as he told Ross, that it was "admirably suitable". It had the very equipment he required and possessed the important advantage of being unknown on the Riviera. It would sail into the port of Cannes an hour or two before it was wanted, its voyage could be kept more or less secret, and it would be easy to ensure that only one man and a boy would be left on board. And, moreover, it could be secured for little extra expense. Relatively, the bunkering would be pin-money, and the owner would be paid no more than the first advance. Anyway, it was Merle-Florac's money, and Merle-Florac, gambling for immense stakes, was not disposed to stint the pennies. Parra went ahead without misgivings.

The whole scheme had seemed to be fool-proof to its originator, and might have been if perverse chance had not intervened. Margolies as well as Flavius was to have been kidnapped, but Margolies had been called unexpectedly to Marseilles just as the zero hour approached. The hitch was bad, but far from disastrous in its immediate consequences. If it had not occurred, Ross would have been left ashore with no Margolies to contradict his puzzling story of charterers who had sailed away without him. This, in the view of Merle-Florac, would have confused the police. They would take some time to see beyond the red herring and suspect that there might be something criminal in the business, and, before they had swung into full action, he would have brought off his coup.

An initial advantage was lost, but the murder of Kane was a far more serious blow, and Merle-Florac, thoroughly frightened, had improvised the ransom touch. At least, this was the assumption, for Parra had had nothing to do with the first demand. According to programme, the captives were to have been released at the end of seven days, but Parra had had the idea of making more money for himself out of the deal, and, with Flavius under hatches, had proceeded to some embellishments of his own.

As Laurent's persistent questioning elicited more and more of the details, Ross listened anxiously, but the end of Jean Seyrac was left untold. Parra and his accomplice in that piece of work were certainly going to keep quiet about it, and apparently the others were ignorant of the second killing. The first informer spoke readily enough of other matters. It was the wounded Hercules who had fired the shots at the escaping Kane. It was Zizi of the *Café des Lauriers* who had collected the ransom on the road to Mouans-Sartoux.

Ross had a conscience to trouble him, but he decided to say nothing about the night in the Rue Tunis. Margolies had been told in confidence, and Margolies agreed that no purpose was to be served by revelation. Only Alicia Mars could suffer if the relationship were traced, and Laurent already had enough to bring against his prisoners.

When they reached Agde, Ralph sent an urgent telegram to his parents and Ross put a telephone call through to Cannes. It was late that night when Max and Ross brought Ralph to the flat in the Rue des États-Unis, but not too late for Ross to go out again on a visit.

Alicia Mars was waiting for him.

Eric Ambler

Doctor Frigo   ISBN: 978-07551-2381-0
A coup d'etat in a Caribbean state causes a political storm in the
region and even the seemingly impassive and impersonal Doctor
Castillo, nicknamed Doctor Frigo, cannot escape the consequences. As
things heat up, Frigo finds that both his profession and life are horribly
at risk.

'As subtle, clever and complex as always' - Sunday Telegraph

'The book is a triumph' - Sunday Times

Judgment on Deltchev   ISBN: 978-07551-1762-8
Foster is hired to cover the trial of Deltchev, who is accused of
treason for allegedly being a member of the sinister and secretive
Brotherhood and preparing a plot to assassinate the head of state
whilst President of the Agrarian Socialist Party and member of the
Provisional Government. It is assumed to be a show trial, but when
Foster encounters Madame Deltchev the plot thickens, with his and
other lives in danger ....

'The maestro is back again, with all his sinister magic intact' - The New
York Times

The Maras Affair   ISBN: 978-07551-1764-2
(Ambler originally writing as Eliot Reed with Charles Rodda)
Charles Burton, journalist, cannot get work past Iron Curtain censors
and knows he should leave the country. However, he is in love with
his secretary, Anna Maras, and she is in danger. Then the President
is assassinated and one of Burton's office workers is found dead.
He decides to smuggle Anna out of the country, but her reluctance
impedes him, as does being sought by secret police and counter-
revolutionaries alike.

ERIC AMBLER

The Schirmer Inheritance   ISBN: 978-07551-1765-9
Former bomber pilot George Carey becomes a lawyer and his first job
with a Philadelphia firm looks tedious - he is asked to read through a
large quantity of files to ensure nothing has been missed in an inheritance case where there is no traceable heir. His discoveries, however,
lead to unforeseen adventures and real danger in post war Greece.

'Ambler towers over most of his newer imitators' - Los Angeles Times

*'Ambler may well be the best writer of suspense stories .. He is the master
craftsman'* - Life

Topkapi (The Light of Day)   ISBN: 978-07551-1768-0
Arthur Simpson is a petty thief who is discovered stealing from a hotel
room. His victim, however, turns out to be a criminal in a league well
above his own and Simpson is blackmailed into smuggling arms into
Turkey for use in a major jewel robbery. The Turkish police, however,
discover the arms and he is further 'blackmailed' by them into spying
on the 'gang' - or must rot in a Turkish jail. However, agreeing to help
brings even greater danger ....

'Ambler is incapable of writing a dull paragraph' - The Sunday Times

Eric Ambler

Siege at the Villa Lipp (Send No More Roses)

Professor Krom believes Paul Firman, alias Oberholzer, is one of those criminals who keep a low profile and are just too clever to get caught. Firman, rich and somewhat shady, agrees to be interviewed in his villa on the French Riviera. But events take an unexpected turn and perhaps there is even someone else artfully hiding in the deep background?

'One of Ambler's most ambitious and best' - The Observer

'Ambler has done it again ... deliciously plausible' - The Guardian

The Levanter

Michael Howell lives the good life in Syria, just three years after the six day war. He has several highly profitable business interests and an Italian office manager who is also his mistress. However, the discovery that his factories are being used as a base by the Palestine Action Force changes everything - he is in extreme danger with nowhere to run ...

'The foremost thriller writer of our time' - Sunday Times

'Our greatest thriller writer' - Graham Greene

42164814R00099

Made in the USA
Middletown, DE
06 April 2017